Why "We" Didn't Choose You
Vol. III
From a Woman's Perspective

Published by ZL Publishing House and Hoston, Enterprises, LLC.

Book Cover Design by Alex Winemiller and Emmanuel Gonzales

A CIP catalog record for this book is available from the Library of Congress.

Hoston, William T.
Why "We" Didn't Choose You, Vol. III

ISBN-10: 0-692-64712-0
ISBN-13: 978-0-692-64712-7

Why "We" Didn't Choose You

Vol. III
From a Woman's Perspective

Edited by
LaTosha M. Duffey
William T. Hoston

CONTENTS

ACKNOWLEDGMENTS

LaTosha M. Duffey

Dear Heavenly Father, I would like to humbly thank you for the many blessings. The blessings continue to pour down upon me. Thank you for taking care of my late grandmother, Norma Jean, and the rest of my family in Heaven.

I want to express my gratitude and love for all of the people who have helped me get to this point in my life. I have a large base of family, friends, and mentors who offer unlimited support to help advance my career. There are so many people who have contributed to shaping, molding, and guiding me in the right direction to achieve all of my goals. I am truly humbled.

I especially want to thank Charlotte Duffey, Jeffery Duffey, Jade Duffey, Jett Duffey, Heir Jackson, Iman Shokuohizadeh, and William T. Hoston.

To you whom I have not named, please know that even though you are not named in this book, I deeply appreciate what you have contributed to my life.

William T. Hoston

All praise to my Lord and savior, Jesus Christ. With Him, all things are possible. He has provided me with the four most influential women in my life, the late Mildred Hoston, the late Bertha-Mae Mitchell, Thelma C. Owens, and Janet Smith. I am a product of their hard work and sacrifice. In the words of Abraham Lincoln, "All that I am, or hope to be, I owe to my angel mother[s]."

To my lovely wife and best friend, Cecilia Hoston, I love you. You have given my life such love, happiness, and joy.

To my son, William T. Hoston, Jr., Daddy loves you. "You keep me smiling/ The things you do for me/ *I Wanna Thank You.*"

We would like to thank the women, and man, who contributed to making this book possible. Thank you from the bottom of our hearts. Each of you provided invaluable input to make this book a timeless piece of art. Second, thank you to all the anonymous readers. Your insight was greatly appreciated and helped contribute to the completion of this book.

INTRODUCTION

This is the final installment of the *Why "We" Didn't Choose You* series. The previous books, *Volume I: A Relationship Handbook for Women (and Men)* and *Volume II: Poetic Love*, have each gained a large fan base of women (and men) around the world who like to read books that dissect the fundamental elements of love and relationships. *Volume III: From a Woman's Perspective* is the crowning piece in the series that gives women an opportunity to voice their opinions on love and relationships and in some ways provides a retort to the men's point of view in Volume I.

Similar to *Volume I*, to begin the process of putting this book together, we recruited women of all races, ages, social backgrounds, educational backgrounds, and relationship statuses. Having a diverse group of women was important to the success of this book. The women provided thought-provoking opinions on a number of central questions that addressed the ever-changing dynamics of relationships.

The goal of *Volume I: A Relationship Handbook for Women (and Men)* was to offer support for women who had lost hope and felt that they would never understand men. The panel of men provided practical information to women to increase their self-awareness in relationships, expand their ability to better understand men, offered information on how to handle conflict in relationships, and gave examples on how to develop an appreciation for the fundamental differences between men and women.

Volume II: Poetic Love was a collection of poems and short stories. The book was written to capture the feelings of happiness, struggle, pain, and love. It contained poems and short stories written from a sense of warmth, emotion, and compassion. Within the pages of the book was a true portrait of the trials and tribulations of meeting a potential mate, falling in love, the good times, the bad times, the ability to compromise, and finding eternal joy.

Volume III: From a Woman's Perspective provides an opportunity for women to explain to men how to create strong, emotional bonds with them to form serious, committed relationships. The panel of women, and one man, discuss their lives and relationships, describe in unison what is needed to satisfy their emotional and physical needs, and shed light on how they maintain confidence in love despite some experiencing disappointment and heart break. Most importantly throughout the book, they provide useful information to men (and women) to increase their understanding of *how* to please a woman.

In chapter one, the women write letters of closure to the men who have broken their hearts. Chapter two discusses what women really want in a relationship. Chapter three focuses on the emotional baggage that women (and men) sometimes bring into relationships and how to prepare for a serious, committed relationship. Chapter four talks about the importance of establishing an equal balance of emotional and sexual intimacy. Chapter five presents an exchange of personal letters from a wife and husband in an attempt to restore their marital relationship. Finally, chapter six contains an ensemble of poems that embody the emotions of the women in the book.

READER SURVEY

1. Are you:

Single ☐ Married ☐ Divorced ☐ Separated ☐

It's Complicated ☐ Dating ☐

Check all that apply

2. On a scale of 1—10, with 10 being the most positive and 1 being the least positive, what role does either religion-faith-spirituality, if any, play in choosing a life partner? **Circle one.**

1 2 3 4 5 6 7 8 9 10

3. What is your age range:

18-25 ☐ 26-34 ☐ 35-44 ☐ 45-54 ☐ 55+ ☐

4. Have you ever been in love? Yes ☐ No ☐ Maybe ☐

If yes, please use one word to describe that feeling:

_____

5. Have you ever been in lust? Yes ☐ No ☐ Maybe ☐

If yes, please use one word to describe that feeling:

_____

6. Have you ever confused lust for love?

Yes ☐ No ☐ Maybe ☐

7. Have you ever had your heart broken?

Yes ☐ No ☐ I Don't Know ☐

If yes, please use one word to describe that feeling:

_____

8. Have you ever broken an individual's heart?

Yes ☐ No ☐ I Don't Know ☐

If yes, please use one word to describe that feeling:

_____

9. On a scale of 1—10, with 10 being the most positive and 1 being the least positive, how important is it to either get married or be married to obtain the ultimate form of happiness in life? **Circle one.**

1 2 3 4 5 6 7 8 9 10

10. Do you believe that you have to be married to "live happily ever after?"

Yes ☐ No ☐ Maybe ☐

11. If you are married, do you have a different perspective? Refer to questions 9 and 10. Yes ☐ No ☐ Maybe ☐

12. What is your greatest relationship concern?

☐ Cheating

☐ Lack of communication

☐ Partner insecurity

☐ Incompatible values

☐ Lack of physical satisfaction

☐ Inability to find a soul mate and/or someone equally yoked

Other _____

Check all that apply

13. List attributes that you look for in a potential partner?

    a. _____
    b. _____
    c. _____
    d. _____
    e. _____
    f. _____
    g. _____

14. Where should a potential couple go out on the first date?

_____

15. What is your main concern on the first date?

☐ It will be difficult to spark interesting conversation
☐ The other person will not think that I am attractive
☐ There will be no type of connection
☐ My expectations will be too high
☐ Their expectations will be too high
☐ An awkward moment will occur
☐ S/he wants to get married sooner than later
☐ S/he will want a kiss
☐ S/he will want a nightcap
☐ S/he will be too aggressive

Other _____

Check all that apply

16. Are you willing to date someone who has been married before?

☐ Yes

☐ No

☐ Maybe

17. Are you willing to date someone who has children?

☐ Yes

☐ No

☐ Maybe

If yes, how many is too many children? _____

Is it important to ask the following questions in the first 90 days of dating:

18. What type of employment field are you in?

☐ Yes ☐ No

19. When was your last serious, committed relationship?

☐ Yes ☐ No

20. How many serious, committed relationships have you been in?

☐ Yes ☐ No

21. Have you ever cheated in a relationship?

☐ Yes ☐ No

22. Have you ever been cheated on in a relationship?

☐ Yes ☐ No

23. How many sexual partners have you had?

☐ Yes ☐ No

24. Do you believe that one partner can satisfy you?

☐ Yes ☐ No

25. Have you told your family and friends about me?

☐ Yes ☐ No

26. What do you like most about me?

☐ Yes ☐ No

27. What would ruin the progress of our relationship?

☐ Yes ☐ No

28. Is there anything about you that I should know, that I do not already know, to make an informed decision about us?

☐ Yes ☐ No

PROFILES OF WOMEN

Angele

Bio: Latina—Late 40s—Single—Elementary Teacher

About Me: I consider myself to be a strong, spiritual woman with a positive outlook on life. I have never been married, and while most women might feel defeated by this fact, I have embraced it. I will not allow marriage to define my happiness. There is no need to live my life wondering "what if . . ." because I'm too busy pondering "what's next . . .". I enjoy traveling and having fun with family and friends. My mantra is that I am a "life-long learner." True to that mantra, I have a wealth of knowledge about a diverse spectrum of subjects— some useful, and some not-that-much. I do not have any children. While I do not have any children of my own, I find myself surrounded by them in my profession. If I have any regrets at all in my life, it's not ever having children.

Preferred Type of Man: The "type" of man who attracts me the most is one with a sense of humor and a kind heart. I cannot date a man who has a bad attitude or a mean spirit. I prefer a man who is witty, well-spoken, and polite in public, but who also has a fun, playful, and a-little-bit-naughty side in private. This would be my ideal partner. I also prefer him to be athletic, spontaneous, enjoy music (all genres), and love kids.

Ideal First Date: An ideal first date would be a pro sporting event, lunch at a beachside café, or a day at an amusement park. In other words, a relaxing setting that lends itself to stimulating conversation and lots of fun.

Alex

Bio: Asian/White—Late 20s—In a Relationship—Ph.D. candidate

About Me: I'd like to think of myself as someone who is currently on a journey towards discovering my "new" self and the universe. I have gotten to the point in my life where I can look back and smile at some of the silly mistakes made in the past. I can honestly say that I have put on a "new" lens to view the world. Looking through this new lens, I am opening myself up to exploring new possibilities, and not remaining hostage to poor choices made in the journey of life—— my form of self-reflection.

I am a gay man. I am open and proud. I love all people unconditionally. I am a very spiritual person. Although some gay people find it difficult to understand queer spirituality, my convictions lead me to believe in a higher power. An important part of my life is my relationship with Jesus Christ. I am a devout Christian.

Preferred Type of Man: I love intelligent men. I have always had a weakness for intelligent men. Generally, I find older men to be more attractive than men around my age or younger. My type is an older, distinguished, professional man who has stimulating conversation. For some reason, I have always believed there is more to gain from dating a man who has more power, prestige, and privilege than I do. I believe in dating up, not down, because of the challenge of always having to grow. This is not to say that I have not dated younger men or those without the above noted attributes, however, I prefer a man who has his sh!t together.

I have typically dated the All-American "white guy" or the more urban-type white guy. However, I do not think that I necessarily have a "race" preference. I believe my past "preference" or "choice" of men has had more to do with location, proximity, and availability. I like men of all shades. I do prefer a man with a muscular build, nice arms, and a clear bulge.

Ideal First Date: The perfect first date for me would be an "all day" date. It would start out going to a nature reserve and partaking in a long walk. I would use that time to really get to know the other person. After the walk, we would likely go to a local art gallery. Following the art gallery, we would go to lunch. I would prefer a place that is very secluded. In this atmosphere, we could get to know each other more and see where the direction of the date is going. Is he feeling me? Am I feeling him? If the date were still going well, then I would suggest going to see a movie. It would be some type of romantic film. Following the movie, I would like to go to a bookstore and talk about the type of life journey he is on, where is his life headed, and what are his life goals. Afterwards, if I liked the person enough, I would invite him back to my house and we would hopefully prepare dinner together. We would enjoy a candle light dinner and wine while listening to classical music. Following the dinner, to end the date, we would go for a walk in a nearby park. Lay a blanket down and sit and watch the moon and stars in the sky. Nature would play us a beautiful lullaby.

Kenndi

Bio: Black—Early 40s—Engaged—Professional Opera Singer

About Me: I am a woman of God, strong, determined, adventurous, loving, compassionate, and affectionate are all adjectives that describe me. I've persevered through life's challenges. Although at times it has been rough, I've never quit. God has been good to me.

I am a professional opera singer and vocal coach. God has blessed me with the gift of song and opportunities to share it all over the world. In these professional roles, I've been able to pursue my dreams and mold young, bright minds.

I enjoy running and have completed numerous races including over 12 half marathons. I love weight-training, powerlifting, and keeping in shape. I'm a novice CrossFit athlete. I enjoy reading everything from my Bible to the latest issue of Essence, Cosmopolitan, or Glamour magazine. I feel it paramount to be informed, as best I can be, in all things political, social, and spiritual. In my library, you'll find books on the histories and theoretical practices of music, developing a more intimate relationship with God, guides to healthy eating, weight training magazines, and sappy fiction love stories! I must admit, I do have a weakness for reality television! But, I figure, life is all about balance and as long as it doesn't consume my day, I can indulge! My family and friends call me the comedian as I enjoy being silly and making people laugh. I am a diehard football fan, and I have a secret desire to one day become an analyst on ESPN!

Preferred Type of Man: The most important thing I prefer in a man is that he has a personal relationship with the Lord. I know that if he truly loves the Lord that relationship will directly reflect how he treats me. I also prefer a man with strong family values, a man who understands his role as the spiritual leader of his family and is fully committed to that responsibility. I favor someone who is physically active. That would allow us to work together in motivating each other to live healthier lives and setting good examples for our future children.

In addition, I am attracted to someone who is goal-oriented, a hard worker, and simultaneously values quality time spent with his family. I am partial to a man who is caring to others, considerate of my feelings and opinions, compassionate to those in need, and can be a comedian when we all need a good laugh! I love a gentle spirit, yet when needed, a man who can take control of any situation. I would love to spend the rest of my life with a man who understands his wife is his partner, and as a team they are working to contribute to their family and society in monumental ways.

Ideal First Date: I prefer that the first date be really light in nature. I would rather meet at Starbucks for coffee or if it's a nice day we can meet in the park. I think the first date should be an opportunity to engage in uninterrupted dialogue. If the first date goes exceptionally well, then I would consider going on a second date.

Camille

Bio: White—Late 30s—Married—Attorney

About Me: I'm just a fun-loving country girl. I was born and raised in the country and moved to the big city for college and remained for law school. I am goal-oriented, hardworking, and have a huge heart. I love everyone. For that reason, a lot of people have tried to take advantage of me. I do not have time for bullsh!t or betrayal. That will only make me be a b!tch. Then, all bets are off. My love for a person goes to a strong dislike.

I'm a working professional by day: business suits, heels, and totally prim-and-proper. After the workday is over, you are likely to catch me in a t-shirt and panties either playing with my kids or sitting on the couch watching all the shows I recorded throughout the week. I work long hours; therefore, I like to relax when I get home. If you met me during the workweek, you would never suspect that I am a laid back person.

I am fiercely loyal to the ones I love. I love my family. I have an awesome husband and two beautiful children. They mean everything to me. I am also close to my mother, brothers, and sisters. We are one big happy family and love each other. That love created a strong foundation for me and has contributed to how I view relationships.

I love to laugh and make people laugh. Life is too short not to enjoy it to the fullest. I create fireworks in everything I do and can't imagine not giving my all at anything and everything I do in life.

Preferred Type of Man: I am a Cinderella story kind of girl. However, I am not the kind with the happily-ever-after, glass slipper crap. I am more like the underdog-conquers-the-world kind, in a tank top, shorts, and flip-flops. I guess that is the rebel in me. For that reason, I prefer a man who is extremely honest. Tell me the truth and let me decide the consequences. I do not intend to tip-toe through life, only to arrive safely at my death. I wanted a man who treated me like a queen.

Check! I wanted a man who was goal-oriented and had his sh!t together. Check! I wanted a man who was capable of loving me unconditionally. Check! I wanted a man who would be a great husband and loving father. Check! I got the man of my dreams. Check!

Ideal First Date: I do not have an ideal first date. I will tell you what we did on our first date. We went to an event called, *Flicked on the Lawn.* We both were in law school together. He had been flirting with me (and some other girls). During this time, he had asked me out a couple of times but I thought he was a player. I would ignore his advances and act like I did not know he was hitting on me. Over time it became apparent that he was really into me. Every time we were around a group of people, he would make me feel like the center of attention. Eventually, I broke down and told him we could go on a date. How he got my attention on the date was the most interesting part. He made dinner for us and brought a nice bottle of wine. My birthday had recently passed so he got me a card and inside the message said it all. He wrote, "Finally." I had a nice time on our first date.

Valerie

Bio: Black—Mid 40s—Married—Engineer

About Me: I am a God-fearing woman, devoted wife of eight years, dedicated step-mother to two young men, and compassionate Gammy of two granddaughters. I am the only daughter to my loving and supportive parents.

Since getting married, I've transformed into a fun-loving domesticator, with a newfound interest and respect for not just cooking, but creating my very own signature soul food dishes. Family and friends appreciate my integrity and are often intrigued by my selflessness. I'm the friend that will cheer you up when you're feeling down, cry with you when you're heartbroken and serve as the butt of your jokes to see you smile. I find myself to be spontaneous and passionate about life. To some, I'm known as a dare devil, willing to try anything at least once. I love to indulge in simple things like riding my motorcycle, impromptu vacations, and catering to others.

I am focused and career-oriented, currently serving as an engineer. I consider myself to be a diligent employee and trustworthy co-worker who strives for excellence and ensures the mission is accomplished in my organization. As a Team Leader, I am hands-on and enjoy working in the trenches rather than serving as a delegator.

My greatest fear is not reaching my full potential or fulfilling the destiny God has in store for me. My motivation is ignited by other's persistency to never allow stumbling blocks to detour them from reaching their goals. This determination inspires me to never give up when faced with my own obstacles. I embrace obstacles and new challenges.

Over the course of my life, I've made lots of mistakes; therefore, I am by no means perfect. I always seek opportunities to improve myself inwardly and outwardly through educational and inspirational training, self-reflection, and self-study of my Bible. My joy comes from seeing others succeed and receive unmerited favor from God. I am easy to please. I love to give without the expectation to receive. If I died today and come back reincarnated, I would return as a never-ending fountain that pours out love because I love to love, and love being in love.

Preferred Type of Man: My preference for a man is quite simple. I'll use the expression that I need a man who is "all that and a bag of chips." However, I desire for his gestures to be rooted in simplicity and sincerity. I prefer a man who is God-fearing, family-oriented, strong in his beliefs (i.e., political, religion) and well-groomed man. I want him to love me unconditionally; and not see my flaws as a barrier, but a work in progress. It is important that he encourages and supports all my ambitions. I want a man who craves quality time with me, not because he has to, but because he wants to; a man who loves to touch and caress me and run his fingers in my hair. He has to be very sensual and sexual— uninhibited and ready at all times. He must be spontaneous. That is a must for me. For instance, if he calls me to say, "Hey Love, I just picked up tickets for a concert and booked us a one night stay at a Bed and Breakfast. So, I need you to put in your leave request, leave work now, go home, and pack a small bag. I'll pick you up within the hour." Our time together isn't forced because he's always creating opportunities to be alone with me. He understands that there is a time and place for everything. Although he's mature, he's willing to go to any extreme to make me laugh uncontrollably.

I prefer a man willing to make decisions as head of household, but not be threatened by my opinions or recommendations during the process. He must be able to effectively communicate and not be afraid to hold me accountable or tell me when I'm wrong. If he doesn't understand me, he doesn't pretend that he does. He also enjoys the quiet time, such as the two of us sitting side-by-side with no words to share, just silence. It is important that he displays his feelings for me and not have a fear of being viewed by others as weak.

Overall, I prefer a man who is strong, grounded in his faith, culturally aware, and well-rounded.

Ideal First Date: When it comes to dating, my imagination runs wild. There are no limits when planning a first date. It could range from a simple dinner and a movie, to an overnight excursion out of town to attend a ballet or a night of drinks, dancing and hot steamy sex.

Well, Here's My Story:
My first encounter with my husband was via phone on November 30, 2006. We were introduced through a (then) co-worker, but (now) sister-in-law because we're married to brothers. He and I exchanged pictures via text and had an immediate attraction to each other. Over the course of a month, we spoke every day. Because we both had baggage, we decided to lay all of our cards on the table to alleviate misconceptions and false representations. Therefore, we spoke candidly about ourselves to include past failed relationships, finances, sexual promiscuity, family dynamics, goals, etc. If you name it, we discussed it.

During one of our many conversations, I mentioned a few things on my bucket list (e.g., horseback riding, going to the mountains, etc).

After a couple of days of conversation, he says to me over the phone, "Let's meet face-to-face." I happily agreed. He proceeded to tell me that he had already planned a trip with three other couples to include his brother and wife, his sister and her husband, and another couple. He booked a cabin at the Blue Ridge Mountains, located in Blue Ridge, Georgia to bring in the New Year with me. Since I am a simple person and easy to please, I was very excited for his thoughtfulness. His attentiveness was refreshing to me because it meant he really listened when I spoke, especially about my bucket list items.

A month later, we met face-to-face at the cabin. My wildest dreams could not compare to the amazing time we shared during that weekend. We went horseback riding, hiking through the woods, etc. The chemistry was so strong that we both could have burst in flames. We couldn't wait to explore each other. We didn't hold back anything. We consummated on our first weekend with each other. Today, there are still no regrets.

Chapter 1

An Open Letter

The beginning of love is to let those we love be perfectly themselves, and not to twist them to fit our own image. Otherwise we love only the reflection of ourselves we find in them. ~Thomas Merton

Open Letter: A letter that is published in a public forum but is addressed to a specific individual or audience. -Merriam-Webster dictionary

In this opening chapter, the panel of women begin with an open letter written to the men from their past. Similar to the letters written in *Volume I*, these letters serve as a bridge to better understand, mentally sort through, put into context, and explain the pitfalls in past relationships. The difference is that these letters were written directly to the men who broke their hearts.

Admittedly, the panel of men in *Volume I* expressed that some of their relationships ended without providing absolute closure to the women from their most substantive relationships. Often times relationships end with no closure. On the short end of the stick are women who are left to ask the questions, "Why did he break up with me?", "What did I do wrong?", and "Why did he choose to break my heart?"

While it is possible to move on without closure, it is without question that closure can bring emotional comfort and a settled mind. There is power in knowing. On the other hand, knowing can lead to an emotional breakdown. The following letters from the panel of women are written to help facilitate emotional closure. Despite some women not receiving closure from their past relationships, their words serve as a form of empowerment to gain the needed closure that has allowed them to move on and establish new, more meaningful relationships without compromising their happiness by holding on to the past.

Angele

Dear Joel,

Do you ever think of us? Do you ever think of me? Do you ever think of just you and me? The way that we were before all the lies began.

You were my world. I loved you more than anyone in this world. I thought you loved me equally. I don't think I will ever be able to understand how a man can say and show his love so openly and convincingly in one breath, and in the next, take that love and squeeze the life out of it with lies upon lies. My grandmother once told me, "Men love to lie." That did not resonate until I met you. "Liar, liar, pants on motherfuck!n' fire!" That is the phrase that comes to mind when my friends ask about you. When my girlfriends and I talk about you, we refer to you as "Mr. Liar."

Case in point: Remember that time I found a used condom wrapper on the floor in your apartment and you concocted a story about letting your married friend use your place to entertain company? Remember that time I found a used pair of panties under your bed and you said it was your ex's? The only problem was that I had cleaned your bedroom several times. Yes, I vacuumed under the bed. Remember your 22nd birthday? I called that morning before class and said I was coming over to cook you breakfast and give you an early birthday present. I was pleasantly surprised to see a woman leaving your apartment breezeway with a plaid black and red shirt that looked like mine, and H&M leggings that looked like mine. When I asked had you seen my shirt, you replied, "No." "Liar, liar, pants on motherfuck!n' fire!"

When I became pregnant with your child, you told me you *did* want a child with me, but the timing was not right. We were young and still in college. You told me your days of playing football and aspirations of going to the NFL would be jeopardized if we started a family at the time. I believed you. Like a fool, I believed you. "Liar, liar, pants on motherfuck!n' fire!"

Two years later, I learned that you already had a child. The baby was just a few months older than the child we would have had. What twisted the knife and hurt me even more at the time was that I found out my dad was terminally ill and would most likely not live to see his grandchildren. Later I found out it would be difficult for me to have children in the future. Not only did I give up my child for you, but my father never got to know my child—his grandbaby! Here I am years later, without a father, without a child, and without the relationship you once convinced me would last forever. You, ironically, have several kids now with several different women and grandchildren to boot. You, who did not want a child, have an abundance of them. I, who has always wanted children—lots, have none. That's an unfair exchange in the name of love.

You not only shattered my heart, but my dreams as well. I trusted you and you lied to me. I remember every time you tore my heart open and didn't care enough to bandage the wound. "Liar, liar, pants on motherfuck!n' fire!"

Alex

Dear Javier,

I remember the way you made me feel when we were happy. I was young, I felt like I had the world in front of me with you by my side. You made me believe that I had the perfect life. After all, who wouldn't want to be in a loving relationship with someone they could trust and were supportive of everything they did? At the time, I knew without a doubt we could see ourselves spending the rest of our lives with each other. We were more than lovers, we were friends. You were my best friend. I loved that I could be both serious and silly, without having to worry about being judged. You made me feel so safe. You made me feel whole. You made me feel loved.

I recollect the ring you gave me. I wore it proudly on my finger, telling the world that I was taken. I was proud to have you in my life.

I thought about you all day. I talked about you all day. You were the first and last thought on my mind. I felt so blessed to be engaged to the perfect man at such a young age. I had never been in a relationship with someone who I completely trusted. No more searching for me. He had found me. God had blessed me beyond measure. Each and every day I wondered how I had been so lucky to find someone like you when other people wait a lifetime and never find that special person.

Having said that, everything you made me believe was a lie. You made me believe you were the perfect man. I had never experienced hurt until you. I gave up a lot of myself to be with you, including going to get a Ph.D. out of state, because you wanted me to stay in the area. I gave up my friends, my time, and mental capacity to see beyond the lies. I am most disappointed that I gave up the person I used to be in order to settle down with you and become the exact type of person you wanted to spend the rest of your life with.

After we broke up, I realized how much you had actually controlled me. I was made to believe I was happy, but honestly I can look back and see my own image in the smoke and mirrors. I was living in denial. I allowed you to have so much control that when we parted ways it was important to start over and re-build my life for me. For that, I can always say thank you because I am a stronger person for it.

I want you to know that I do not hold any resentment toward you. Upon reflection of our relationship, I was only in love with the image that you made me believe was you. You did me a favor by lying to me. You did me a favor by hurting me. You helped me understand that pain can be a gift. I am back to myself again, the me before you, and it feels good to be able to be happy all over again. I wish you happiness. I wish that some day you become an honest man. I wish for you to find someone who you can love unconditionally without having to lie to them. When you eventually find that someone, I wish the two of you the best.

Kenndi
Dear Lincoln,

I hope this letter finds you doing well and on the restoration side of life. Since you and I do not have a vested interest in each other's lives (i.e., a reason to ever speak again), I will use this opportunity to speak my peace and say my farewell.

Let me begin by saying, I don't hate you. I hate your actions. I hate that you are a liar. I hate your bad decisions. I hate your bad ways. But because of my relationship with Christ, I don't hate you. If I held hate toward you, then I would be hypocritical in my religious beliefs. Now more than ever, you should read that book I gave you, *The Purpose Driven Life*.

When we first started dating and both noticed there was a connection, I remember that I remained a little reserved and continued to hold up my guard. I told you that I was "pumping my brakes." Your reply was, "If you pump your brakes and I pump my brakes, it will lead to stagnation." *Do you remember that?* You encouraged me to "let my foot off of the brake" and allow myself to feel and totally embrace how I felt about you. Little did I know you were a D.U.I.R. waiting to happen— driving under the influence of reckless. When I took my foot off of the brake, you put the pedal to the metal. I was loving, compassionate, and faithful in our relationship. And you were a low down dirty dog— unfaithful on every level.

After we decided that our attraction for each other was leading us to a relationship that now incorporated sex, I told you I had many concerns. I don't take having sex lightly. I explained to you that if I decided to become physically intimate with you, it was because my feelings for you were in a place where I would be seeking a serious, committed relationship. Your reply to me was that you felt the same way about me. *Do you remember that?* I told you that I hadn't had sex in over a year. In true ventriloquist fashion, you spoke in a way that made it seem like the words were actually coming from your heart. You assured me that the last time you had sex was almost a year as well because you had been

5

very busy with life and didn't participate in casual sexual relationships. I remember thinking to myself, "This is a good man!" Not only did you lie about not having sex in almost a year, but I later found out that you slept with more than twelve women when we were together.

I think that if you are going to continue to be a low down dirty dog, you should consider the following: 1. Never leave a digital trail. Emailing is not a good idea. There is an essential folder in your email system, it's called the "trash" bucket. Move all emails there and permanently delete them. 2. Don't talk to women who know each other from college. Facebook suggests us all as friends. Who is Kirsten anyway? She keeps requesting me. 3. Tell your friends to stop posting pictures on Facebook of you around other women. I do have 20/20 vision. 4. Buy a headset for your cell phone. Twice you called your other female friends and mistakenly merged us all on one call. 5. Delete Tinder from your cell phone. No man in a serious, committed relationship should have the Tinder application on their phone. 6. I saw your profile on *PlentyOfFish* (POF). What grown man names his profile, "MakeHerFeelGood69"? You couldn't even make me feel good!

You are a very skilled con-artist. You deserve an Oscar for best actor in a leading role. And the Oscar goes to, "Low Down Dirty Dog!" But one thing is for sure, I'm not going to allow you to change who I am. I'm not going to become the person who believes that "all men are dogs and liars." Though many of them are, I still believe there are some good men who still exist in this world.

Camille

Dear Blake,

I find it funny writing this letter to you after so much time has passed. Yet, I am writing to you nonetheless. I know that we've discussed our failed relationship many times before, but the one thing that has never been said is, "Thank you!" Thank you for freeing me! Thank you for letting me go! After looking back over our relationship, I had to finally admit to myself that I did not have the strength to let you go. I could have never ended the relationship. The reality is that I was so caught up in you, in us, and in the thought of what our relationship could (and would one day become), I abandoned myself for your love. I no longer loved myself. I only loved you. I just wanted us to stay together through the lies, cheating, and hurt. From the bottom of my heart, I have to thank you for ending the pain because I had grown numb to it.

Please understand that I am not putting all the blame on you. I know that I was closed off at times, and it was difficult for me to express my love for you. Sometimes I tried a lot. Sometimes I tried a little. Sometimes I just didn't try at all. There were times when I knew you needed me, but I just didn't know exactly what you needed or how to give it to you. I was younger than you, and I'm sure that my immaturity showed quite often. In the beginning, you gave me a lot of love, but I had no idea how to love an older man. In the beginning, you demanded reciprocity, but I had no idea how to make an older man feel loved. In the beginning, you wanted to teach me how to love you, but I was too naive to understand your intentions. Therefore, I will assume half of the blame for my part in not giving you the love you deserved. I just wish you had stayed dedicated to the relationship.

Towards the end of our relationship, and for a long time afterwards, I was very angry and bitter by the fact that you seemed to not care about me. You cheated on me, though you never admitted it, and I remained with you. I was hurt. I was conflicted. I was in love. But since I had not adhered to your emotional needs in the beginning of the relationship, I blamed myself for your actions. That was my mistake. When I was ready to please you in every way possible, you seemed to be simply going through the motions. Our love became very chaotic. However, I continued to love you "not in spite of, but because of." I thought you were going to be my forever love.

That was all then, and this is now. Today, I have forgiven you for all the pain and hurt you caused me in our relationship. It took some time and a lot of self-reflection. I got over the extreme dislike I had for you after we finally called it quits. Forgiving you allowed me to trust and love again. I could not allow anyone else into my life until I had totally forgiven you. Once I did, it restored my faith in love and relationships.

I am still a work in progress because God is not finished with me yet. Presently, I'm blessed with a happy and healthy family, and I don't regret anything that I went through to get to this point in my life. I pray that you are well and that you have found your true love.

Valerie

Hello Ethyn,

It was great seeing you the other day. Really, it was just so refreshing. I'm only sorry we didn't have the opportunity to really sit and chit-chat for a longer period of time. There is still so much to say after all of these years.

Hey, do you remember the verse to our favorite song by Luther Vandross?

"Don't you remember you told me you loved me baby, you said you'd be coming back this way again, babe. Baby, baby, baby, baby, oh baby, I love you, I really do."

Wow, just seeing you bombarded my mind with so many memories. I know you probably think that I'm going to say something nice about those memories. But, I am not. I'm referring to the memories that have haunted me. The memories that I wish to forget, but every now and then subtle things cast a reminder. These lingering memories at one point were painful reminders of my past.

You were eleven years older than me. I had the wrong perception about dating an older man. I thought I would learn from you how a man should really treat a woman. I was wrong. What I learned is all of the ends and outs of your confidential secrets and lies. There were times when I would watch you sleep and wondered how you could be at such peace with all the bullsh!t you dished out. Even when we frequented the church, I never understood how you could stand, rejoice, praise God, and even cry on occasion, when you were such a whoremonger. How many women did you tell, "I love you" when we were together? How many women did you give your time to, which should have been reserved for me, when we were together? How many women did you have sex with when we were together? You cast a deceitful web. In the words of Sir Walter Scott, "Oh, what a tangled web we weave . . . when first we practice to deceive."

I must take some accountability for my actions. I, too, am responsible for allowing you to cast me in your deceitful web. It started as a loving, deceitful relationship. But in the end, I stayed for the fringe benefits. I was your trophy and that came with an expensive price. I fell in love with the shopping sprees, fine dining, trips, concerts, and surprise gifts. But as the old adage goes, "Free, just ain't free." I found that out the hard way. Every time I tried to leave, you would surprise me with an expensive gift. It was the "yo-yo" effect.

It did not take long to figure out your pattern. You operated on guilt. If you gave a woman your phone number or vice versa, you would buy me flowers. If you spent time with another woman, you would take me out to dinner. If you had sex with another woman, you would buy me an expensive gift. If you took another woman on a trip, you would, in return, take me on a trip. You cheated on me. I used you. I thought that would make us even, but it did not. Do you realize how frustrating it is to know the truth about someone, yet you have convinced yourself that the situation has more pros than cons? Let me tell you, it's very hurtful. I knew the filthy truth, but stayed and tried to live a clean lie.

The lies turned into bitterness. Bitterness turned into paranoia. Paranoia turned into jealousy. That jealousy was my breaking point. I would sit in your home while you were out entertaining other women. The final straw came when you arrived home after a business trip with plane tickets for a vacation in the Bahamas and a rose color Hermes Birkin bag. There was joy and pain in the moment. After all the cheating, I was no longer capable of being in a relationship with you.

Today, I am married to the man of my dreams. You know the *man* that little girls read about in books, they begin a family, and it leads to a happy ending. God has truly blessed me.

Chapter 2

What Do Women "Really" Want?

I, with a deeper instinct, choose a man who compels my strength, who makes enormous demands on me, who does not doubt my courage or my toughness, who does not believe me naïve or innocent, who has the courage to treat me like a woman.
~Anais Nin

Trust: Assured reliance on the character, ability, strength, or truth of someone or something. -Merriam-Webster dictionary

What do women "really" want in a relationship? *Trust.* Women want to be able to trust their partner. Building and maintaining trust is an important element in a relationship. When trust is not one of the founding principles, the relationship will endure unnecessary ups and downs. In a new relationship, it is imperative to create a firm foundation to build trust. In an existing relationship, trust must be the anchor to keep the relationship from moving in the wrong direction.

This chapter investigates whether women believe that "all" men cheat and the implications of cheating? As we all know, cheating breaks the bond of trust. One of the most difficult hurdles to cross is rebuilding trust in an existing relationship once the bond of trust has been broken. The panel of women will talk about the following questions and offer their insight: Do you believe that "all" men will cheat? How did being cheated on emotionally affect you? Have you ever cheated? Have you considered cheating?

Will "All" Men Cheat?

Angele

The short answer to this question is, "No". I *do* believe that it is in a man's nature to cheat, however, I personally do not assume that *all* men will cheat.

In my 30 plus years of dating, I have yet to discover a man who does not cheat. But I never approach a relationship assuming that he will. To assume that all men cheat would make for a miserable relationship that would be doomed from the get-go. It would be like assuming that all women are gold diggers. That is not true. What relationship could survive believing that it's only a matter of time before the man cheats? That constant thought would fuel the inevitable.

In general, I have a rosy perspective on relationships. I would like to believe that my father was faithful to my mother. I would like to believe that my grandfather was faithful to my grandmother. They were married for 72 years. Therefore, being faithful is a part of my core belief when in a relationship.

As rosy as my perspective is on relationships within my mind, I am not naïve nor victimless to cheating. I have been cheated on multiple times. Throughout my life, I have entered long-distance relationships that have been difficult to maintain. I have to admit, long-distance relationships are tough. Many days and nights are spent alone. The main components to keeping the relationship thriving are making frequent trips, trust, and setting realistic expectations. When the trips become few and far between, the trust breaks down and the expectations dwindled. I knew when each one of my ex's was cheating, especially the last person I dated. He stopped accepting my calls at all times of the day. He made excuses as to why he could not FaceTime me. He blocked me from his Instagram page. The icing on the cake was when he cancelled two trips in a row. I asked him point blank, "Are you cheating on me?" His response was, "I think we need to move on." When you reach my age, not a lot needs to be said at the end of a relationship. I do not require an explanation. If you do not want to be with me, I can accept that. All that I ask for is to be a man and not a grown boy.

Alex

I do not think that all men will necessarily cheat, but I think a lot of men have the tendency to cheat. American society has made it too easy and acceptable for men to cheat. Unfortunately, I also think a lot of men measure their sense of masculinity by their sexuality (i.e., how much sex they can get and from how many different people). In our society, men are welcomed to be sexual predators (within reason under the law). They are often excused from being monogamous. On the other hand, women (and gay men) are constantly ridiculed for their sexual behavior and deemed promiscuous.

I do not think all women assume all men will cheat. I do think that women who assume all men will cheat have some valid reason(s) to believe so. Although I am not a woman, my experiences with men have been consistent with women who have been cheated on and now are cautious in relationships. For instance, I was involved in a love triangle years ago with a man who was dating me and another woman. He thought he could have his cake and eat it too. Wrong! On his birthday, we both showed up to his job to surprise him. Surprise! His secretary knew about the woman he was dating but did not know about me. The other woman had arrived before me. She had bought him a pair of Salvatore Ferragamo moccasin loafers. Surprise! I bought the same loafers. When the secretary told him he had a visitor, the office door opened and he had the happiest smile on his face, which was a residual from his interaction with the other woman. The problem was, I knew that smile. I had seen it before. I had placed a similar smile on his face. I quickly scanned the office and saw a Ferragamo shoe bag on his desk. Wait . . . What . . . No he didn't! Did he tell us both to buy him the same gift. I 3D scanned the entire room and could tell you complete measurements. When he saw me, the gay inside of him jumped out of his body and ran down the hall. There stood the shell of a cheater. "Sir, I will be with you in a second," he told me. Wait . . . What . . . No he didn't! I handed my Ferragamo shoe bag to his secretary and walked out. After about ten steps, I made a legal walking U-turn and retrieved the shoes from his secretary. What was I thinking? I'll answer, I wasn't.

I headed back to Nordstrom and got a refund. I then proceeded to use the emergency credit card he had provided me and bought a Burberry watch, Burberry belt, Burberry wallet, and a pair of Burberry boots. For good measure, I bought a bottle of Creed Green Irish Tweed. Surprise! Emergency!

Kenndi

The logical part of me finds it difficult to make a blanket statement using a quantifier such as "All." My mind says that each man is an individual and there are plenty of men out here that respect their wives, fiancées, and girlfriends. He values her health and his own. He would not expose her to deceit or sexually transmitted diseases. My logic says that he respects their relationship and finds nothing more valuable than the sanctity of being faithful because of his love for her. Thus, he would never jeopardize the wellness of their relationship. The rational side of me says that most men, although they have eyes and can admire another woman's beauty, only has eyes for the woman he has given his heart to.

Using this logic, I want to believe that before he does anything that would put his relationship (or family) at risk, that he will think about the effect that it may have on the future of their endeavor together. All of these things are what I would like to believe. They are what my mind tells me. My mind wants me to be sensible. My mind tells me that this is what I should feel. But the reality of it all is that, I don't. It is because of past experiences, and not just of my own, but also through the observations of my friends and women in my family. Most of them have experienced their significant others engaging in affairs, including my father. My mother has always told me that every woman has her limit and at some point she must decide what she will tolerate and what she will not. Some women turn a blind eye knowing that their significant other is sleeping with someone else. Other women chose to confront the situation and even after he has confessed, they decide to stay. But every woman has her limit.

Entering relationships, I hoped and prayed that my significant other would respect me enough and value the relationship enough that he would choose me (and only me). That's really all any woman ever wants. Although I'm hoping and praying that he will refrain, my heart repeatedly tries to prepare myself for the moment when he does step out on the relationship. In my last relationship, I was visiting my boyfriend during Christmas as we lived on opposite ends of the country. While I was there, I found a card from another woman that said, "I love you and I love being with you. We are perfect together, Kim." Even though he hadn't previously given me reason not to trust him, seeing that card was almost a release of a known emotion because I felt like it was confirmation and he had finally lived up to what I anticipated. He repeatedly tried to reassure me that it didn't mean anything. I didn't end the relationship at that particular moment, but I no longer felt secure in the relationship. If he didn't call, in my mind I believed it was because he was with her. He let me know that he felt I didn't trust him anymore and I couldn't deny it. I no longer trusted him. I expected him to do what I believed that all men would eventually do. Disappointingly, he did it. To answer the question, although I can't speak for all women, I can say that I do believe that all men cheat.

Camille

No. I think that a lot of women assume all men cheat, however, there are some women who believe that men only cheat for a reason. I can't say that I've ever felt like *all* men will cheat. I have, however, been at the point where I felt like it was an insurmountable task to find a man who would not. For me, all it took was being cheated on once to question the character of every other man I encountered. After being cheated on for a second time, I decided that relationships were not for me for an extended period of time. I didn't have the time to try and figure out who was a "good guy" versus a "bad guy." A lot of women are victims to the act of cheating. If not, it has happened to some other women who they know. We all internalize each other's feelings. Good or bad, that is what we do. Once the seed of concern is planted that it is likely he will cheat, it doesn't need much else to grow. In certain instances the concern grows like a Bamboo tree, which is problematic and makes it difficult for women to trust and engage in a healthy relationship with a man.

Most women would agree that all men are *capable* of cheating. This means that they have a natural propensity to be attracted to and desire to be with other women. Still, a lot of other factors play into whether or not they will act on those desires (e.g., faith, morals, values, character, fears, opportunity). Let's be completely honest, *some* men are just dogs and will take advantage of any opportunity that presents itself. I once dated a guy who was a real dog. We weren't even in a relationship, yet he flirted with all of my friends (sometimes right in front of me). Needless to say, he had sex with three of my so-called friends when we were dating. He was handsome, very charming, nice physique, and well-endowed. After he had sex with the first woman, she told another of their sexual exploits and it snowballed to three. It really didn't matter because I wasn't into him. However, the thought of him telling me how much he liked me and wanted to begin a relationship with me was mind-blowing. What an asshole?!

Still in all, there is that small minority of women who continue to believe there are good men in the world. They are the hopeless romantics, the forever optimists that see the good in all men and don't think that it will ever happen to them. God bless them!

Valerie

It is definitely a strong assumption for women to believe that all men will cheat. However, in most cases, the majority of women do assume that all men will cheat. This assumption generally stems from their experiences with a cheating man, either personal (direct) or from someone else's experience (indirect). For example, perhaps their husband, boyfriend, or significant other cheated on them. Or, maybe they witnessed the cheating from their grandfather, father, brother, uncle or cousin. Or, maybe the cheater was some other male figure they had held in high regard such as a pastor, favorite professor, politician or mentor. Or, maybe they themselves are intimately involved with a married man.

Women are built on emotion. One of the strongest emotions a woman feels is love. When a woman loves, she loves hard. To love hard means going to any extreme to ensure that her partner is satisfied, going the distance to protect that relationship, and sometimes sacrificing her own self-respect. Another valued emotion is trust. When a woman trusts, she does it whole-heartedly. That trust is usually very genuine and sincere. As a consequence, a woman's world is shattered when that love and bond of trust is broken. That feeling of hurt often leaves a woman feeling embarrassed, ashamed, and inadequate. In some cases, her feelings manifest into insecurities that have the ability to plant a seed of low self-esteem.

I, too, experienced being cheated on by a man who I believed loved me. I was embarrassed. I was ashamed. I felt inadequate. I didn't expect it nor did I see it coming. I dated a guy who started out as a platonic friend. He then turned into my best friend. He came from a good family and we both shared in having our parents being married 30+ years. Thus, I believed he knew the value of being faithful in a relationship. Against our better judgment, we decided to take our friendship to the next level. As most people do in relationships we set parameters to love each other unconditionally, be monogamous, and maintain the foundation of our friendship.

During the first six months of our new relationship, things were going very well, or so I thought. After about nine months, things started to drastically change. We weren't communicating as much and when I asked him about it, he would get frustrated. Eventually, the forced and limited communication became hostile. Soon enough, our relationship was on a downward spiral. I tried everything to save the relationship, but it was hopeless. I honestly cannot pinpoint when and how things got so bad. Then one day, he called to end the relationship.

About a month later, I found out from a friend that he had gone back to an ex-girlfriend who was five months pregnant. I was mortified because not only did I lose my boyfriend, but I lost my best friend. In my heart, I believed he was such the perfect guy for me. As I mentioned before, he came from a good family with a devoted father. I was confident that the type of family he observed growing up would have an influence on our relationship.

I never thought I would be able to get past the hurt, betrayal, deception, and lies. I was more embarrassed that others knew of his infidelity, the other woman, and their expected child. Since that time, I have had many other relationships. Have I encountered other cheating men? Absolutely. Having said that, in spite of these experiences, I do not believe that all men will cheat.

The Emotional Effects of Cheating

Angele

For the most part, I have been guarded in all of my relationships. Let me explain: As a little girl you wait to have your first boyfriend. Imagine the thought of finally being able to experience dating, having a crush on a boy, and falling in love with him. Then that fantasy is crushed when he cheats on you. Puppy love hurts. Adult love hurts. Love just hurts. While I understand that certain expectations are unrealistic for young girls, it does set an emotional foundation. Take for example, my very first boyfriend cheated on me. I was devastated. I was not mature enough to understand that this was "par for the course." For that reason, I will remember him for the rest of my life. When I reflect, the first thought is that he cheated on me. That's the way my dating life began, being cheated on.

It took me a while to show my feelings in the second relationship. I was afraid he would do the exact same thing. As described in my open letter, after years of being in a relationship and loving him unconditionally, I discovered that he had a child with another woman during our relationship. Wow! I fell back into the same funk believing that I was unworthy, inadequate, and ugly.

After that failed relationship, I decided to throw myself into my work and began to think that perhaps love would just 'happen' for me when I least expected. Five years later, I reconnected with a male friend who I had considered dating in the past. The only reason I did not move forward with dating him was because at the time he was in the Navy and relocated to Japan. Before leaving, he poured his heart out to me and asked me to go with him. I honestly considered it. However, my father had recently passed away. Due to that, I could not leave my mother and family.

This man seemed so genuine and loving. Since I had not been in any kind of a relationship for a long time, I pursued the relationship with everything I had only to be let down in a *huge* way. I discovered he was also dating a woman 20 years older than me! Being dumped for a senior citizen by a man who claimed to love me so deeply just hit me in the face like a ton of bricks. I was absolutely devastated.

Here is the part where most women would just give up on ever finding a "faithful" man. I could have legitimately thrown in the towel and accepted that *all* men cheat! Or, I could chalk it up to another life experience. I decided that I would not let these men (whom some I still love very much), skew the way I view *all* men. I had the best male role model in the world, which was my father. Because of his presence in my life, I *know* that men can be faithful and loving toward one woman. Personally, I just have not crossed paths with him yet.

Alex

To my knowledge, I have only been cheated on twice in terms of physical intimacy. Even in the story described earlier, he vehemently denied having sex with her. I have, however, caught previous partners emotionally cheating, which is worse.

For instance, I caught a previous partner on a dating website and I felt very betrayed. I did not feel that it was my fault nor did I feel a sense of inadequacy. I interpreted it as I was dating a liar and someone who may have potential to be a cheater. Therefore, I had two choices: 1. I could accept it and worry about him eventually finding someone else. 2. I could confront him and he lie to me about *why* he was on the site. I chose the latter. I asked him about it. He apologized. I initially accepted that he was sorry. But after that incident, he never deleted the account. I became very suspicious of his actions. Soon after, I found out the password to his email account where a duplicate email from the dating site would come. I started monitoring his emails to find he was communicating with another gentleman. To make matters worse, he was communicating about me. He told this complete stranger everything about our relationship. In one email exchange, he said, "I love him, but he does not make me happy." That hurt.

I have been involved with different men since that relationship. Although I try not to let my past relationships influence my current relationships, I would be lying to say they had no effect. I have a hard time trusting people, and completely letting my guard down. I am always a little suspicious that someone is doing something that they are not supposed to be doing. I hate that because I have been with some really good guys who have never cheated.

The emotional impact of being in a relationship with a liar sets the stage for emotional turmoil. You begin to think that all men are liars and instead of letting the relationship happen naturally, you come into the relationship with a set of suspicions and assumptions. You are always guarded. I keep my heart very much guarded. Even though I am working on it, I really never let my guard completely down. When a man who you love dearly has hurt you, it is hard to believe that other men will not do the same thing.

Kenndi

Often times, as women, our esteem coincides with how we are viewed and treated in a relationship. If a man is good to us, we believe it's because we make him happy. If he is faithful, we feel that it's because we've "earned" that treatment. In contrast, when he cheats, unfortunately, it's the same. We feel that he cheated because we were *not* good enough or we *have not* earned his complete love. The way we feel about ourselves is based on the way "they" treat us, and that's unfortunate. It takes an emotional toll on us and we begin to question our self-worth. We ask ourselves questions like: What did I say? What did I do? Am I no longer attractive? Am I not satisfying him sexually? What is it about me that would cause him to cheat? We own his actions, and in turn, it relieves him of having to take responsibility.

Over the course of my life, I can think of two instances where I found out that someone I was dating was cheating. As described in the last response, I was in a long distance relationship visiting my boyfriend over the Christmas break and found a card from another woman. The card ended, "We are perfect together, Kim." I broke up with him and allowed them to be perfect together. The reason I reintroduce this incident is because she used the word, "perfect." As a woman, I know many times for us to use specific language to describe our relationship with a man there has to be certain words said, certain actions performed, and certain feelings evoked. "We are perfect together," is a powerful statement.

The second instance was discussed in my opening letter. The guy who I was dating was simultaneously seeing multiple women. One day he left his email account open and one of the other women copied and pasted dozens of messages involving multiple women into one long email and forwarded it to all the women in his address book. The message even went out to his mother, sisters, and supervisor at work. The subject line read, "Mr. Cheater." He was telling all of us how much he loved and cared for us in the same exact words. I met him at church in the Single's Ministry. The pastor introduced us one night after the sermon. It was the pastor's endorsement of him that led me to date him. He was a "Low Down Dirty Dog!"

I later found out after we broke up that two of the women were pregnant, one seven months and the other three months. Expectedly, I was hurt beyond words. More importantly, I couldn't believe that another human being would hurt so many people with no regard. As one can imagine, after an experience like that, there was nothing a man could say or do for a long time to convince me that he'd be any different. As time moved on, I did heal and accepted that all men aren't like that. I understood that I could not allow my past to affect my present and future. There are some good men out there who deserve a fair chance.

Camille

I have been cheated on twice (that I personally know of). Both had different effects on me. The first time, I was young, only 18 years old. Of course it hurt, but I remember getting over it quickly. I guess I was in what my mother calls, "Puppy love." We had dated throughout high school, and were really good friends. Once we went off to college the relationship and our approach to the relationship changed. It just wasn't the same anymore when we would see each other. I confronted him because I felt the difference in the relationship. I asked him, "Are you seeing someone else?" He replied, "No." Then I asked, "Have you cheated on me?" He answered, "Yes." Even more disappointing, I knew the person who he cheated with. It was a friend from high school who went to the same college he attended.

The second situation was a whole different story. I went through a lot in that relationship as noted in my opening letter. I can't even describe in words how much it hurt. I was an emotional wreck for a long period of time. It made me question myself. What did I do wrong? Could I have done something to prevent it? How long had it been going on? One of the hardest things about the situation was that he wouldn't admit that he actually cheated on me. Oddly enough, since he wouldn't admit it, I wanted to act like he didn't either. That was a stupid decision.

At the time, we were in a long distance relationship. It was late one night and I had called him several times. Each time the call went to voicemail. The power of my intuition made me get into the car at 3 a.m. and drive four hours to check on him. I knocked on the door. He asked, "Who is it?" I said, "Me." Ten minutes later he opened the door. Then another woman appeared seemingly coming from the bathroom. He introduced us and said it was a childhood friend who was passing through town. She had a few too many drinks, became drunk, and he let her spend the night on the couch. In complete shock, I did not question the story at the time and she left. When I finally came to my senses, I asked a slew of questions. Why didn't you tell me she was in town? *I don't know.* Why was your phone off? *The battery died.* Why did it take you so long to answer the door? *I panicked. I knew how it would look.* Where did she sleep? *She slept on the couch.* Did you have sex with her? *No!* Are you lying to me? *No!* His story was complete and utter bullsh!t and I bought it. All because I loved him and wanted to keep him in my life.

When the relationship finally ended, I was an emotional wreck. I entered the blocking code *67 to call him to just listen to his voice. I wrote him emails but let them remain in the draft folder. I wrote him handwritten letters but did not send them. I wanted him back but I no longer trusted him. To make matters worse, I did not trust myself to be able to choose a good partner to move on. I allowed the situation to emotionally break me down. Over time, I started dating again. However, it was for entertainment purposes only. I wasn't looking for a relationship; I just wanted someone to hang out with. Anytime someone started to get close, or expressed having feelings for me, I would pull away. The pain of my previous relationship haunted me for years.

Valerie

How did being cheated on emotionally affect me? Well, my first thought was, "Will I ever get past the hurt, betrayal, deception, and lies? Second, I began to ask the questions, "why, what, how, who"? Why did this happen to me? What did I do wrong to deserve this? How could I be so stupid to allow this to happen to me? Who can I trust? Will I be able to ever trust again? Sometimes, it's hard to pick up the pieces and "keep it moving."

As a woman, I am an emotional creature and very passionate about life. What that simply means is, I love to love and be in love. I love very hard. How do I measure loving hard? I compare it to loving someone unconditionally. I love their flaws and all. Sometimes I criticize myself for this level of emotion. At one time, it was one of my biggest flaws. In past relationships, that kind of love made me vulnerable to cheaters. A cheater isn't always as good as they think. Often times, the "red flags" are present before the cheater is caught or confesses to cheating. Because I loved so hard, I ignored the signs for fear of being alone or not finding another man to love me, which stemmed from low self-esteem and confidence.

In my opening letter, I explained how I dated an attorney who was eleven years older than me. He was the first guy I had dated with a significant age gap. We worked together at the same law office. I was his paralegal and had access to all of his personal items and passwords. I ended the opening letter explaining how his level of guilt equated to buying expensive gifts and taking me on luxurious trips. The final straw came when he arrived home after a business trip with plane tickets for a vacation in the Bahamas and a rose color Hermes Birkin bag. I knew he had gone on a romantic getaway with another woman, yet disguised it as a business trip. My thought process, although flawed, was to go on the trip and end the relationship when we returned. We never went on the trip because I saw him having sex in his office with another woman. Yes, I saw him. About two weeks prior to our trip, he was preparing for an important case and asked me to bring certain files home to review. On the day of this observation (for lack of a better word), I forgot a key file at the office. He was in meetings all day and was supposed to be having drinks with the fellas later that evening. When I returned to the office, I heard two people talking in his office. The door was slightly cracked open. As I was approaching his office door, the talking was replaced with the sound of kissing. I peeked through the crack to confirm. He was kissing her, unbuttoning her blouse, and unzipping her skirt—— all in one motion. As soon as I walked away, I heard the sound of penetration. She inhaled and I exhaled.

From this situation I learned that I could not love someone else without loving me first. I learned how to indulge in myself, spend time with myself, and most importantly, appreciate myself. I was able to open up and be honest to myself. I developed respect for myself.

Have You Ever Cheated?
Have You Considered Cheating?

Angele

Yes. When this question was posed, I had to think long and hard because I am *not* the cheating "type". At the time that it happened, I told myself that it wasn't cheating because he had done it to me. However, I knew in my heart that it was cheating. Let me explain the situation:

It was football season. My boyfriend was a star player for the local college. During the season, I discovered he had cheated on me. He got a lot of attention from the women on campus and cherished every moment of it.

One night some friends and I were at a party across town at a beach house. Little did we know it was being hosted by a few of the guys from the rival football team. I had several friends on both teams. Most of them I knew from growing up in the area. One of the players from the rival team had had a crush on me for a long time. In fact, he had been trying to get me to go out with him unbeknownst to my boyfriend. Each and every time I told him, "No!" They were actually acquaintances with mutual friends. Therefore, they knew of one another through friends and by playing football against each other.

To make a long story short, I began drinking and got a bit carried away. We had made eye contact earlier in the night but I tried my hardest to avoid him. After a few drinks, I saw other girls at the party that were talking to him. Because I knew he had a crush on me, I made myself visible–—- very visible. I remember thinking that if my boyfriend can just have sex with someone else without regard for my feelings, why can't I? Why can't I have sex with this guy with no emotional attachment? After a while, we locked eyes and he came over to talk to me. He was 6' 4", olive complexion, muscular body, big arms, hazel eyes, and had succulent lips. "Can we go outside and talk?" he asked me. I did not utter a word. I followed him outside.

We walked along the beach and talked for about an hour. Then we found a remote spot and started making out. I could tell he had longed for this moment. He was gentle, attentive, and made sure he pleased me. It was a break from the "Wham! Bam! Thank you ma'am" that my boyfriend had grown accustom to giving me. He explored places my boyfriend did not know existed. For him, my body was a part of a treasure hunt. His mission was to find the hidden pearl.

The next day, I felt a rush of guilt. I was certain my boyfriend would find out because he was friends with some of the players in attendance. Either they didn't tell him or he knew but chose not to confront me. I will never know. At the time, I was honest with the other guy by telling him that I was not going to leave my boyfriend. In hindsight, he might have been the better choice. Over the years, my boyfriend continued to cheat on me. And to think, I felt guilty for a one-night stand.

Alex

Hmmmmmm. This is a good question. To continue from the previous response, I have cheated. When I started monitoring my partner's emails from the dating site and found out he was communicating about me, it led me down an unforgiving road. I am not making any excuses for my actions but I only cheated after observing a very explicit email. I confronted him about it, and of course, he denied engaging in certain actions.

I had been friends with this other guy for years. I always knew he liked me. However, I did not feel the same way about him. He would invite me to dinner, to movies, to concerts, etc. He was adamant about dating me. When I found out my partner was being dishonest, I contacted him. We only had one special night. But, I felt liberated.

I am in a relationship with someone now. He is a really good guy. I have never considered cheating on him, but there are times that I think about other guys. I do not think I would act on those thoughts. The older I become, the harder it seems for me to be really committed to someone. I think maybe because I am always looking for something better. Age has the ability to make an individual constantly question whether they are wasting their time in a relationship. When someone stops becoming a source of inspiration and/or motivation for me, I become less interested in them. I start seeing other men that appear to be more fascinating and that is a problem for me. It has nothing to do with being more physically attracted to someone else, it is the emotional aspect that is most fascinating. I ask myself: How will this other guy make me feel? Can he help me unveil untapped potential?

Attraction is a powerful emotion. I do not believe in acting on my feelings. I do not want to hurt someone in a way that men have hurt me. Having said that, I do want to find a partner who will satisfy my emotional needs.

Kenndi

I have never physically cheated on a boyfriend. I believe that sexual relations create soul ties and I am very protective of my body and who I invite into my soul. It takes a long time for me to develop a level of trust with a man to proceed with a sexual relationship. Thus, to finally establish that connection, I would not enter into another sexual relationship with a man under any circumstances. I realize that many people do not put as much weight on sexual relations as I do and count the experience as an aspect of temporary physical joy. I, on the other hand, regard it as much more than just a physical activity and believe sex to be the highest level of emotional connection.

I have emotionally cheated on a boyfriend. While in a past relationship, an ex-boyfriend started reaching out to me. We began talking on the phone often and engaging in conversations that would not be reflective of a woman in a relationship with someone else. I do not think my boyfriend at the time would have been pleased if he heard some of the things we talked about. The conversations were descriptive and rekindling old feelings, yet I cared deeply for my current boyfriend. However, there was a soul tie to the past relationship that I just could not let go of, which affected me. I often felt guilty when I got off of the phone with him, especially if my boyfriend called immediately after to talk. The tones of the two conversations were vastly different. I would even replay our conversations in my head while I was in the company of my boyfriend. I felt terrible. Here I am an advocate of staying faithful and being respectful of my mind and body, and I let an ex-boyfriend mind f!ck me. It felt so good at the time. It didn't matter that I wasn't having sexual intercourse with him because I was letting him re-enter my life. That was worse. Every action has a reaction. I ended our conversations and recommitted myself to the relationship with my boyfriend.

Camille

I have never cheated in the physical sense, but I have considered cheating. I never acted on the thought simply because I'm just not that type of girl. It's hard enough for me to be with one person physically, therefore, it is not physically (nor emotionally) possible for me to be with two people. More importantly, I have never wanted to allow a situation or person to push me to the point of doing something out of my character.

With that being said, I still considered cheating. After I found out my boyfriend had cheated on me, I wanted to get back at him. I thought that it might somehow make me feel better. I wanted revenge!

I am of the belief that cheating can be both physical and emotional. To that end, I have cheated in the emotional sense. It was with the unlikeliest of people: my best friend. My best friend is male. Needless to say, my boyfriend hated that. My boyfriend would always say, "He loves you more than just a friend." I would dismiss the thought. Then one day, I confided in my best friend about all the problems going on in my relationship. In mid sentence, he stopped me and said, "I love you too much to allow you to go through this." I kept talking because he always told me he loved me. He stopped me and said, "Did you hear what I said?" I replied, "Yes, I know you love me and care about me." He then made it clear, "No, I love you. I am in love with you. I have always loved you." I was in shock. The thought of us being together had crossed mind, however, I did not want to jeopardize our friendship. We had been friends all of our lives. I paused for a second and replied, "I love you too." I had been fighting it, but the feeling was mutual.

My best friend did something that my boyfriend did not do. He listened to me! We would talk for hours without noticing how much time had passed. I became completely comfortable with him and began to confide even more things to him that I never told anyone. Before long, I needed to talk to him. I needed to be around him. I needed to be in his arms. He would come over and hang out all day. We enjoyed each other's company more than before. The surprising thing is, we never acted on our feelings, and eventually we decided it was best to remain in the friend zone. I wasn't ready to end my relationship with my boyfriend, and it wasn't fair to my best friend to wait for me.

Valerie

Have I ever cheated? Well, if I said, "No," I would definitely be lying. If I said, "Yes," I'd have to add that I've cheated more than once. In my opinion, I had valid excuses for cheating: 1. I cheated to get even with my ex-boyfriend(s). 2. I cheated because I was just not that into my boyfriend. 3. I simply had to have the other guy. Maybe all of them aren't valid excuses, but they were the excuses I used during those periods in my life.

Cheating to Get Even with Boyfriend (s):

I worked as a lead paralegal at a law firm. This law firm is different than the one previously discussed. I was assigned to one of the partnering attorneys. About three months into this new job, we started dating. We'll call him "Mr. Legal." Our relationship was never really about sex. He was a religious man. Mr. Legal went to church every Sunday, attended Bible study, mentored young men at the church, and delivered meals to the elderly. Despite his love for God and the church, Mr. Legal was a religious playboy. All of his church-related activities made him popular with the women in the church. I soon found out that he was seeing another woman in the church. He camouflaged their relationship by telling me repeatedly that he was only giving her spiritual counsel due to the fact she was going through a rough time in her life. Well, he was giving her more than counsel.

After my suspicions were confirmed, I figured what was good for the goose was damn sure good for the gander. As that cliché became my motto, I began to regularly hook up with an ex-boyfriend. We'll call him "Mr. Tax Accountant." One day while at Mr. Tax Accountant's place getting my annual taxes prepared, we began to stroll down memory lane. The conversation became pretty heated between us. I said, "Ummm, maybe it's time for me to go!" He too agreed. As we walked towards his front door, he grabbed me and turned me around so that my back was to him. First, he hugged me from behind and kissed my neck. He then pulled up my dress and snatched my panties off. Right then and there, we re-kindled the physical part of our old relationship. Not once, did I think of Mr. Legal. Was I wrong? No. In my mind, he had it coming.

Not That into My Boyfriend, Had to Have the Other Guy:

I loved "Mr. Macho." He was the perfect guy. Mr. Macho was bitterly divorced with two daughters. He had the 3C's: his own *Car*, his own *Crib*, and excellent *Credit*. There was only one problem, Mr. Macho wasn't sure that he wanted to get married again. We dated for 2 ½ years. During this period, I asked myself, "Where is this relationship going?" We had multiple conversations about marriage, and at the end of those conversations there was still ambiguity. To make matters worse, Mr. Macho had incorporated a lot of rules into our relationship. His failed marriage left him with control and trust issues. For instance, he said, "Although we're in a monogamous relationship, you still can't just show up to my house unannounced." Wait . . . what? I couldn't visit with him on Sundays during football season. I couldn't visit him while his daughters were visiting for the weekend. I couldn't leave any items of clothing at his house. There were rules, rules, and more rules. For the longest time, I accepted his rules because I loved him. However, with little hope that our relationship would blossom any further, I eventually became frustrated, irritated by all the rules, and bored. I was not that into Mr. Macho anymore.

That coming summer I decided to enroll in a summer school class to finish up some required electives in my graduate program. On the first day of class, this one guy caught my eye. We'll call him "Mr. Scholar." Actually, he caught my eye up until the last day of class. During class, I would daydream about us hooking up. He appeared to be very quiet. I figured since he hadn't approached me that maybe he had a girlfriend. But, it really didn't matter to me. I had my eyes set on him; and I knew one way or the other, we would eventually hook up. I wondered how I could get him to approach me or vice versa. One evening after class, we shared an elevator and had the opportunity to make small talk. I told him I was headed out of town for a work convention. We both alluded to maybe hanging out upon my return. Well it didn't happen, at least not right away. Prior to summer school ending, I solicited his assistance for our final class project. He agreed to review it and provide feedback. We made plans for me to meet at his place.

When that day came, I showed up in my favorite, sexy sundress with the split up the thigh. The exact same one I'd used to tempt and seduce Mr. Macho. Initially, things started out professional. Mr. Scholar was really critiquing my project. He wanted me to do well in the class. That actually turned me on even more! I repeatedly had to go to the bathroom because my panties were soaking wet. After the third time, I took my panties off and placed them in my purse. My imagination was running wild thinking about the things I could do to Mr. Scholar and with Mr. Scholar. Finally, as we were wrapping up the important stuff, he excused himself for about five minutes. When he returned, Mr. Scholar asked me to follow him to his bedroom. When he opened the door, the room was lit with candles, rose petals covered the bed, and chilled bottle of wine set on the nightstand. All I know is that Mr. Scholar went from professional to nasty in the blink of an eye. It was amazing.

When I left there, I felt so guilty. I was actually in love with Mr. Macho. Yet, I couldn't stay away from Mr. Scholar. Because Mr. Macho was unavailable on Sundays due to football, I made sure to meet with Mr. Scholar. He taught me all about football—— the X's and O's, the strategy, and the various positions. Mr. Scholar played quarterback. I played center.

Hooking up with Mr. Scholar opened my eyes to what was really happening in my relationship. I was in no way ready to stay committed to Mr. Macho. Eventually, I ended our 2 ½ year relationship. To this day, I still feel guilty for cheating.

Chapter 3

Don't Judge Me, Love Me

I'm selfish, impatient and a little insecure. I make mistakes, I am out of control and at times hard to handle. But if you can't handle me at my worst, then you sure as hell don't deserve me at my best. ~Marilyn Monroe

Transparency: Free from pretense or deceit. -Merriam-Webster dictionary

The art of transparency is invaluable. The ability for an individual and/or couple to be honest and open about their feelings will have a powerful effect on the lasting nature of the relationship. On one hand, transparency opens the door for criticism. On the other hand, transparency opens the door for empowerment. If two people want to meet each other's emotional needs, there must be a certain level of emotional honesty that is communicated from their willingness to be transparent. The willingness to be completely honest helps to resolve conflict in relationships. Failure to disclose feelings, address the source of the feelings, and talk to resolve any conflict, is detrimental to the continual growth of the relationship.

This chapter focuses on baggage in relationships, and the importance of overcoming baggage to create healthy relationships. The panel of women will discuss the following questions: What baggage and/or flaws do men possess? What do women need from men while in a relationship to satisfy their emotional needs? Why do women stay in relationships after being hurt?

1 Carry on + 1 Personal Item

Angele

I personally don't like to carry preconceived ideas about people before getting to know them. This is simply because I realize that all people have flaws, and likewise, all people have some innate goodness in them. Drawing from my own experience, I suppose the biggest gripe I have regarding men is their ability to lie, even in the face of truth. "Liar, liar, pants on motherfuck!n' fire!"

If a man is "caught" cheating, he will still deny any wrongdoing. Or, he'll try his damnedest to sway you to believe that he loves you and has absolutely no feelings for the other woman. When you asked him, "Why did you stick your d!ck in her?" His answer will be, "I don't know. I had a moment of weakness." To that, I say, "Liar, liar, pants on motherfuck!n' fire!" Just be honest guys!

Take, for example, I was dating a guy and every time I went to his apartment to pick him up, his roommate would ask, "Are you Maribel?" Who the f!ck is Maribel? Why would his roommate be so disrespectful? One day, I met Maribel. Yes, we did favor each other in a lot of ways. The guy I was dating told me Maribel was just a co-worker. He lied. "Liar, liar, pants on motherfuck!n' fire!" Needless to say, I allowed him to lie to me to keep him in my life. This was a byproduct of my low self-esteem and self-confidence at the time. "Liar, liar, pants on motherfuck!n' fire!"

The most disturbing part of this story is that his roommate kept asking me, "Are you Maribel?" Why would his roommate be so disrespectful? Ladies, let me tell you why this little prick would be so disrespectful. When a man frames you in a disrespectful manner to his friends, they will treat you accordingly. As women we need to pay less attention to the words our partners say and greater attention to how our partner treats us around his family and friends. Observation is realization. I realize this circumstance varies from relationship to relationship. However, in most cases his friend is a great barometer to identify whether the man you are dating is vested in beginning a serious, committed relationship with you.

Alex

From my experiences, there are a couple of commonalities that I believe most men possess. The first one is, I believe a lot of men have been emotionally hurt in relationships. Society has conditioned men to not express their vulnerable side. Therefore, these men are reluctant to acknowledge their feelings outwardly, and instead, they deal with their feelings inwardly. They hold on to this baggage and it makes many men develop a negative disposition toward a potential partner, even when courting in the beginning of a relationship. We fall for this type of treatment because we realize he has been broken by a past relationship and we think we can fix him. It is not my job to fix a man. There is not that much Gorilla Glue in the world. Humpty Dumpty fell off the wall for a reason! They couldn't put Humpty Dumpty back together again. Some of these Humpty Dumpty's play the role of victim and end up victimizing us.

The second one is, I believe that a lot of men are more sensitive than they would care to admit. This is not a bad thing. It only becomes a bad thing when they let their emotions build up over time due to a string of bad relationships. There is often this idea that men do not keep tallies and can easily move on from relationship to relationship. This is not true. I once dated a man who cried on my shoulder about all of his heterosexual relationships. He had recently come out of the closet. I was his first gay love. Our problems arose when he brought his heterosexual insecurities into our relationship. He began to accuse me of being dishonest, cheating, and contemplating to end the relationship. Wait . . . Wait . . . One damn minute! I am not being dishonest. I am not cheating. I am definitely not contemplating ending the relationship. His package was too good to end a good relationship prematurely. I sat him down and openly communicated my feelings for him. He cried like a baby on my shoulder.

Kenndi

What baggage and/or flaws do men possess? A lot! To begin, a man will shift the blame to a woman. More often than not, women are labeled as the partner in the relationship that comes with the most baggage. Anytime we feel hurt or betrayed or angry, it can never be merely an expression of our feelings toward the current man we are dating. In most cases, the man who we are dating will shift the blame to the ex-boyfriend. I've had a man say to me, "Your ex-boyfriend must have really hurt you?" My reply was, "No, you are just an asshole!" Men love to "blame shift." That is one of my pet peeves. The same man said to me, "If you didn't make me so angry all the time, I wouldn't yell at you." Hold on Mr. Angry man! I am not the root of your anger.

In general, what people fail to realize is that men have just as much baggage, if not more, than women. Combining the reasons of an absent model of a successful marriage, failed past relationships, the negative influences of peers, and being overworked and underpaid, every day life can be difficult for some men. As the saying goes, "What worries you, masters you." The stresses and demands of life often find their way into the relationships. Unfortunately, most men are reluctant to admit when the world is on their shoulders. When the weight becomes unbearable, they lash out against the world. In many cases, it is the person closest to them—— their partner. On the other hand, when women are confronted with the same stresses and demands and they eventually lash out, men think it's because she is a "bag lady."

Finally, I think another common form of baggage comes from the disappointments of failed past relationships. In the game of relationships, most of the time men are kings and women are pawns—— much like chess. Men prescribe the type of moves that will occur in the relationship. In chess, the king serves as one of the most important pieces. He, as well, is one of the weakest. The king can only move in one vacant space at a time, but in any direction. Therein lies the problem for two reasons: 1. The king takes forever to commit to a move. 2. If the king is under attack (i.e., feeling insecure, afraid of commitment, or wants to end the relationship), the next move is to protect himself from being attacked (i.e., cheating or abruptly ending the relationship). This leads to a failed relationship (on his part). When the man decides to enter a new relationship and problems arise, he reflects on the "why, how, and what would have happened if . . ." of the past relationship. Why did we break you? *Because of you.* How did it end? *You ended it.* What would have happened if we stayed together? *You will never know.*

Camille

I love, love, love a confident man. As much as I love a confident man, there is a fine line between confidence and arrogance! Arrogance is one of the biggest character flaws for men. I have found that many professional and highly educated men fall into this category. The difference between the two (for me) is that a confident person is secure in who they are and their abilities. In contrast, an arrogant person feels superior to others because of their abilities. I have dated a couple of arrogant men. As a result, I have developed a disdain for them. I often felt like they were trying to belittle others and me. I'm just a fun-loving country girl. I've done well for myself, but I am very down to earth. Arrogant men make my skin crawl!

The other deal breaker is dating a mama's boy. Ugh!!! I love family, and I speak with my mother on a regularly basis, but there are limits. There needs to be some separation. I dated a guy for about one month, which was all I could take, who talked on the phone with his mom daily, visited with her several times a week, and she would come over to his house and do his laundry and wash his dishes twice a week. That is too much. To be fair, she was a very sweet lady, but her involvement in his life was excessive. The funny thing was, he got very defensive when I asked him why his mother was so involved in his daily life. He didn't see anything wrong with how his life revolved around her. The last straw was when she asked to have a private discussion with me. We went into the backyard and began to chitchat. Her exact words were, "How is the sex with my son?" Huh . . . Wait . . . Did she . . . Yes she did . . . Did she mean to . . . I think she did. I asked, "With all due respect, what do you mean?" She began to explain to me that he broke up with his last girlfriend because the sex was bad. Wait . . . Am I having this discussion with his mother . . . Yes I am . . . With his mother of all people . . . Jesus make it stop. My reply was, "I do not feel comfortable having this discussion." Then she proceeded to say, "If you need any tips, let me know." Oh hell no! I can remember thinking, I wish I was invisible right now. Jesus, please make me invisible. Needless to say, that was one of the longest months, four weeks, and 30 days of my life.

Valerie

In retrospect, men are no different than women when it comes to relationships. Just like women, men get hurt, used, and abused. They often carry baggage from relationship to relationship (just as women do). It is highly unfair to place all of the onus on women being the ones who bring baggage into the relationship.

Too many times, we've heard the saying, "Hell hath no fury like a woman scorned." Well, I beg to differ. There is nothing worse than a scorned man. With a scorned woman, you never have to wonder why she's angry or who's wronged her because she is forthcoming about her pain. However, with a scorned man, he's too macho and prideful to admit that he's been hurt. A man will hide his disappointment, hurt, and pain with a smile. Or, a man will cover up his pain with multiple sexual partners. The adage goes, "You get over someone by getting under someone else". This is only a temporary fix. The pain is still there.

In my current relationship, I am married to the man of my dreams. He is my prince charming. He loves me unconditionally without hesitation; and he loves me not because he has to, but because he wants to. He loves me on purpose. Like me, he has imperfections. Nonetheless, I love him like a tarnished brass trumpet that still plays the most beautiful tune. He is the melody of my life.

Prior to our union, my husband was married for almost 21 years. He acknowledges that he should have left after the first six years. But he stayed. He stayed for his sons. He stayed for his family. He stayed for all the wrong reasons. He stayed to please everyone except himself. In the end, staying was a detriment to his psyche. After his divorce, he vowed to never marry again. He became the poster child for a bitter divorce. My husband was single for five years until he decided he was ready to date again. We met and married rather quickly after only dating for a short stint.

My husband shared with me some of the details from his dark and painful marriage. One of the things that affected him the most was that his ex-wife was blatantly disrespectful and challenged his manhood. Very soon after we became engaged, I started to see his baggage. For example, he called off our wedding two times. Why? The first time was because I responded to him in a condescending tone. Although I was joking, he saw it as a sign of disrespect and reverted back to the memories of his previous marriage. He vowed to never allow any women to disrespect him again. The second time was when I was visiting my parents for the holidays. I met up with a girlfriend for dinner. He assumed I was out with one of my ex-boyfriends. Why? I have no idea.

After we got married, the smallest arguments would lead him to threaten to pack my things and move me out of the house. The first three years of our marriage were rough. We argued. Let me rephrase that, we argued "A LOT." We argued because each of us became poor communicators. We argued over almost everything. The only thing we did not argue about was sex. Thank God for that! We argued before sex. We argued after sex. We fell into a space where sex was our only positive form of communication.

It took a lot of counseling to get beyond that point in our marriage. In the end, all worked out for the best. Why? It was because of love. We both loved each other and did not want to give up on the marriage.

How to Satisfy a Woman's Emotional and Physical Needs?

Angele

Emotionally, my needs as a woman are multidimensional. To begin, I want to feel loved. I do not want my partner to only tell me he loves me. I want him to show it through his actions. The older you get, words have no context without action. A man wins a woman's heart through his actions. That is the bottom line.

I want to see and feel the love when he hugs me, kisses me, cuddles with me, or cooks a meal for me (in his boxer briefs). I want him to make me laugh. I want him to comfort me. I want him to listen to me. I want him to console me. I want to be able to cry on his shoulder. I want to cultivate a level of reciprocity where there is a mutual exchange of emotional needs.

When it comes to my physical needs, I want to feel safe in his arms. Whether we are out on a date or in the bedroom, I need my man to be the right balance of good and bad. I want him to hug me like it is the last time. I want him to kiss me like our lips were born to be together. I want him to make love to me like he loves me and hates me. I want him to fulfill my every desire.

If my emotional and physical needs are not being met, we should discuss the gap in the relationship. If it continues, the only alternative is to step away from the relationship. As a single, 40-something year-old woman, it is imperative for me to be with a man who is willing to meet my emotional and physical needs. It takes time to meet such a man. On one hand, time is of the essence. On the other hand, everything takes time. I absolutely do not want to give my love and attention to the wrong man during a lonely time. I have done that before.

As I get older, my biggest fear is to die old and lonely. This fear resonates mainly because I gave my younger years to men who were not deserving of my love. I developed a high tolerance level for hurt, pain, and disappointment. Because of this, in my later years, there is a growing fear that my best days are behind me.

Alex

I feel that my most emotional needs revolve around the ability to express my autonomy in a relationship. I want to feel accepted. I want to feel respected. I want to be valued. Having said that, I do not want to feel controlled. Because I have dated older men in the past, they felt it was within their right to control me. They did not accept me totally. They did not respect me totally. They did not value me totally. I was just their P.Y.T. (Pretty Young Thing).

When my emotional needs have not been met in a relationship, I find myself spending a lot more time by myself. It is in this space that I can sort through the priorities of the relationship. I call it the "break before the break." Oddly, the two parties in the relationship know when the end is near. Before one person makes up his or her mind to end it, there is a "break before the break." Some refer to it as "being distant." This period can be emotionally draining. Should I break up with him? Should I remain distant to make him break up with me? Should we have a conversation that will ultimately lead to a break up? This pivotal stage in the relationship is nerve wrecking.

For instance, I once broke up with a man over Skype. Yasss . . . I said . . . Skype! The relationship was in shambles prior to the breakup. When he came over, we always argued. When we hung out, he was boring. When we talked on the phone, there was silence. When we had sex, he would go soft. Yasss . . . I said soft! I respected him too much to break up over the phone or via text message. I was afraid to break up with him in person. He was a very intimidating man. As a happy medium, I chose Skype. I texted him and asked could he Skype me. On the video call, I expressed the need to move on. He listened and did not say one word until the end of the call. Before getting off, he said, "I respect your decision. I have to be honest with you. I've been dating someone else and didn't know how to tell you." The F!ck!

Kenndi

As a woman, my emotional and physical needs are directly related to my spiritual needs. There are certain characteristics that God instilled in women as human beings that should guide our lives and set a standard when considering the courtship of a man. I believe in the words of Maya Angelou, that "A woman's heart should be so hidden in God that a man has to seek Him just to find her."

I desire the need for unconditional love. I desire the need for emotional support. I desire the need to be nurtured. Most importantly, I desire a man who possesses the ability to touch my heart, as well as, touch my body in a way it has never been touched before. While this description may automatically lead one to think about sex, there is so much more to physical stimulation than just the act of sexual intercourse. I, by nature, am a very affectionate person and the art of "touch" is very important to me. When I'm with my partner, I want to be in constant physical contact with him. If we are walking in the park, I want us to be holding hands. If we are lying on the couch, I want our bodies to touch in some shape, form, or fashion. If we are in bed, I want him to be cuddling me. In fact, I find these forms of touching more emotionally stimulating than sex.

If these needs are not being met, I'll communicate to my partner how important these forms of "touching" are to me. Physical touch is my love sign. He needs to know and understand that. Once he knows what is important to me and if he is still unable to meet those needs, it may be time to reevaluate our relationship.

Camille

My top three emotional needs are respect, trust, and love. For me, all three of these emotions go together and build upon each other. I have been in relationships where I received one, maybe two, but not all three and that was an issue. For example, if a man disrespects me, I am not inclined to believe that he can be trusted and that trust leads to love. These emotions are key to a healthy relationship.

I once dated a man who was disrespectful toward my desire to achieve an advanced degree. During my first year of law school, I went on a couple of dates with a man I met at the grocery store. He was attractive, had never been married, no kids, worked at the post office, and was very nice at first. After a couple of dates, I realized he was intimidated by my ambition to pursue a law degree. He would always say or ask the most demeaning questions. For instance, when we had a disagreement, he would say, "This is not a court room", "I'm not one of your clients", or "Ok, your Honor." He was unwilling to encourage meaningful growth in my life. Instead, he tore me down with his words in an attempt to control and marginalize me in the relationship.

The sh!t hit the fan when he asked me one day, "Don't you think that a woman is better suited to be a paralegal than a lawyer?" Bye! No . . . Really . . . Bye! I will not tolerate a man who is threatened by the growth of his partner.

From a physical standpoint, I need affection and sexual fulfillment. Unlike my emotional needs, I can't say that any one of these needs is a deal breaker. This is because I value emotional needs more than physical needs. Don't get me wrong, I need affection (e.g., hugging, cuddling, kissing, and hand holding). However, I do not place a requirement on how much my partner hugs, cuddles, kisses, holds my hand, and makes love to me. I would rather feel his emotional love more than his physical love. Men are masters at giving physical love. But as women, we should demand them to be masters at giving emotional love as well. When we do not, we often mistake physical love for emotional love. This is one of the biggest mistakes that women make in a relationship.

Valerie

I am emotionally built. I love to love. I love being in love. I love catering to my partner. A part of my joy comes from seeing my partner happy. The other part comes from my partner taking the initiative to give me the same type of love that I give to him.

As a woman, my basic emotional and physical needs are intimacy, open communication, affection, quality time, validation, sense of security, and more importantly, love. For me, the emotion of intimacy is defined as, "In-to-me". Before giving myself to someone else, he must be in to me and not only wanting to be inside of me. Intimacy takes place over time and is the guiding force in the development of a serious, committed relationship. It is the building block. Next comes communication.

In my marriage, open communication is not an option but a priority. It allows me to stay connected with my husband: his thoughts, his concerns, his problems, and whatever may or may not be affecting the growth of our marriage. Communication is more than words: it is verbal, mental, and physical. When in unison, the art of communication sustains the relationship. For example, when my husband is having a bad day, I listen to his story, read his mind, and observe his body language. I am attentive to his needs. In return, he is attentive to my needs.

My husband gives me unlimited affection. Despite our busy schedules, we make quality time for each other. He validates my existence and gives me a tremendous sense of security. More importantly, my husband gives me love. It's very genuine and sincere. Like I said earlier, the first three years of our marriage were rough but we worked through the challenging times. I learned that anything worth having is worth working for.

When a woman's emotional and physical needs are not met, it causes problems, disappointment, insecurity, and frustration. Before getting married, when my needs were not met in a relationship, I would seek fulfillment in another man. I wouldn't communicate with my partner nor make any demands in the relationship. I would sacrifice my own happiness until I became frustrated with him, the dysfunction of the relationship, and anything that would remind me of how unhappy I had become in the relationship. Today, there is no other alternative to fulfilling my needs. I'm more vocal and make it a point to share my thoughts and concerns with my husband. In return, he does a great job at listening, providing assurance, and making me feel that I am the apple of his eye.

I Continued to Be with You . . .

Angele

I continued to be with you after you hurt me because I did not want to be alone. I should have ended the relationship sooner, but I thought you were the key to my happiness. I couldn't bring myself to end the relationship because I didn't know how to live without you. You treated me bad! You cheated on me! You were an asshole to me! But, I stayed. I was afraid of being alone. I was afraid of feeling like a failure. Like they say, "One more love, one more heartbreak." Instead of conceding you treated me bad, I made it a point to be the perfect girlfriend, hoping your behavior would change. Instead of conceding you cheated on me, I made myself even more vulnerable trying to compete against women whom I had never met before. Instead of conceding you were an asshole and ending the relationship, I stayed.

I kept a diary back then. Over the years, I have looked at the entries from our relationship. Let me read one of them:

> A heart can only break once. On the second and third time, there is only a sudden stop in blood circulation— cardiac arrest. A beating heart signals survival. A broken heart challenges a woman to love herself.

> I am lost in a world that does not exist. I use the fantasy to deal with the reality. I use the reality to deal with the pain. That is the only way to survive a broken heart.

Alex

I continued to be with you after you hurt me because during that time I thought I loved you and you loved me. I should have ended the relationship when I found out that you were a compulsive lair. To borrow from Angele, "Liar, liar, pants on motherfuck!n' fire!" Do not fuck!n' lie to me! I am a human being with real emotions and feelings.

The primary reason I stayed in the relationship was because you had a huge emotional stronghold on me. During our relationship, you were a master bullsh!t artist. My love sign is words of affirmation. Boyyy . . . Did you take advantage of that sh!t! You would constantly tell me, "I love you, Alex. You make me so happy. You have the best moonchie in the world. I can't imagine my life without you." You had me wide open, literally and figuratively.

It normally takes a lot for me to fall completely in love with someone. I fell on my face for you. I was very naive. When I thought that your words were as pure as a nun on her deathbed, I later found out that you used your words as a weapon against my innocence. You stabbed the sh!t out of my heart. You were married and did not tell me. You were living two lives. You were spending time with your family and me. You were having sex with your wife and me. You were having heterosexual sex and gay sex. Boyyy . . . You are a deceitful, trifling, insignificant, nasty, tiny d!ck bastard!

I loved you. I really loved you. I loved you enough to act like I was one of your business associates when your wife visited our table at Pappadeaux Seafood Kitchen while having a celebratory lunch with her friends on her motherfuck!n' birthday. I remember it like it was last night at 6:39:03 p.m.—— down to the second! I said to myself, "Who is this woman approaching our table?" Then she spoke. "Honey, I didn't know you were going to be here for lunch," she said while leaning down to kiss you. "Wait . . . B!tch . . . Who are you?" Those exact words ran through my mind. "Alex (who has the best moonchie in the world) and I are grabbing a bit to eat before heading back to work," you responded in disbelief that your cover was blown. I politely excused myself from the table, headed to my car, and drove the f!ck off. On the way home, I called you everything but a child of God. Boyyy . . . You taught me a valuable lesson. One of the best ways to avoid a broken heart is to pretend that you do not have one.

Kenndi

I continued to be with you after you hurt me because I allowed my love for you to trump the love I should have had for myself. Had I had resilient faith in God and believed all the good things He created within me, I would have never ignored His warnings. During that period in my life, I had reached an all-time low. I had invested so much time, effort, and energy into our relationship, I could not give up. I did not understand that there is a difference between giving up, and knowing when to walk away to maintain your morals. I didn't want to lose all that I had given, not realizing that I had already lost.

I should have ended the relationship after I realized that things would not get any better. The first time I caught you in a lie, I should have believed that you were a liar. The first time you called me a b!tch, I should have believed that you were a disrespectful man. The first time you hit me, I should have believed that you were incapable of loving me. But instead, I chose to believe that the man committing these acts was not you. I told myself that everyone makes mistakes. I told myself to be strong and courageous. I told myself that God wants me to fight to make this relationship work. I put words in God's mouth. He then spit them out.

I was wrong, yet I chose to stay. The emotional stronghold you had on me compromised my ability to reason. Men always say that women are crazy, but never take responsibility for driving us crazy. In our relationship, I was unable to think and behave rationally because my thoughts, my actions, my being, were tied up in pleasing you. "Love is patient." Is love really patient? I spent a lot of time exercising my patience in a relationship that was headed into a dead end. Women often abide by the following phrases, "To love means to endure", "To love means to tolerate", and "To love means to lose yourself." While all these things are true (to an extent), it should never compromise 'who you are' and 'how you deserve to be treated' by a man.

Camille

I continued to be with you after you hurt me because I was young, naïve, and very much in love with you. I believed that if I stayed with you, it would be different *from that point forward. From that point forward* came and went, came and went, and came and went. There are only so many times that a couple can start over. *From that point forward* eventually became the point of enlightenment.

I really wanted the relationship to work. I believed in you. I believed in us. When things were good, they were really good. You made me feel like the most important person in the world. I had never been with someone who made me feel the way that you had made me feel. You supported my dreams. You fed words to my soul. You made love to my mind. At the time, I thought that you made my life better.

I should have ended the relationship after you encouraged me to get an abortion. How could someone who once made me feel like the most important person in the world now make me feel worthless? Having an abortion was one of the biggest mistakes of my life. During that time, I wish that I had been a stronger person. I wish that I were a fraction of the woman that I am today. The months following the abortion changed my life, my perception of myself, my perception of you, and my perception of us. Yet, I forgave you and continued to love you. I pushed my family away and ended friendships because I could not stop loving you. More importantly, I lost myself.

I continued to be with you because I loved you. I fell in love and stayed there. Thank you for leaving me where I fell.

Valerie

I continued to be with you after you hurt me over and over again because I was young, dumb, and full of cum. I was blinded by the idea of love. You put me on a pedestal. But the higher you placed me, the higher your bullsh!t rose. Soon after, I could smell the sh!t every single day.

I should have ended the relationship after you threw my sh!t out of your house. What man throws a woman's personal items out of his house when he is the one who is caught cheating? I can't believe the unmitigated gall of you to cheat with "our" personal trainer. She was having sex with you and training me. I do appreciate the fact that you folded my things, placed them in a nice suitcase, and sat the luggage on the front porch. When I forgave you, you placed all my items back in their original place.

Maybe I should have ended the relationship when I discovered your dirty little secret with a stripper. You had a stripper at the house, gave her money that could have been spent on me, and then filmed an explicit sex tape of her performing oral sex on you. Who does that? What kind of man are/were you? Let me answer. You are a professional man who hides behind his tailored-made suits, Stefano Beyer shoes, Rolex, Ferrari F430 car, and big house. What kind of woman was I at the time? *I was a person who wanted security. I was a person who fell for a man who promised me the world. I was a person who enjoyed the finer things in life.* I later discovered that everything that glitters is not gold.

Luther Ingram once sang a song titled, *If Loving You Is Wrong*. The lyrics went, "If loving you is wrong/ I don't wanna be right/ If being right means being without you/ I'd rather live a wrong doing life." I chose a wrong doing life. During our time together, I developed so many toxic behaviors. One of them was being afraid to leave your presence in fear that you would immediately go and entertain another woman (or stripper). This is why I wanted us to spend the entire weekend together, each and every weekend. For a brief period, I even stopped going to church on Sundays. I found a couple of old fashion bobby pins on the bathroom counter one Sunday afternoon. When I asked you about them, you said you had bought them to clean your ears. Wait . . . What WTH! Does this guy think that I am crazy? *Yes.* Does he think I am "Boo-boo the fool"? *He must.* I knew that if I spent the entire weekend with you, no one else would be there. This provided a 48-hour peace of mind. My motto at the time was, "It's better to have a piece of a man than no man at all."

Luckily for me, I got the help I needed to break from your emotional stronghold. With help from my parents, girlfriends, and a counselor, I was finally able to free myself from the illusion of happiness. I renewed my faith with God; and vowed to never idol a man and his material possessions ever again in my life. As I began to heal, I took accountability for the error of my ways in the relationship. I accepted my flaws. Once a woman has accepted her flaws, no one can ever use them against her.

Chapter 4

Making Love > Sex

No act can be quite so intimate as the sexual embrace. ~Havelock Ellis

Love Making: The act of making love. -Merriam-Webster dictionary

The act of making love is a process that takes emotional and sexual intimacy. This act first begins with an emotional attachment between two people. After a period of time, hopefully this growing emotional attachment will lead to them falling in love with each other. This will establish a heightened level of emotional intimacy, which should be the prerequisite that leads to sexual intimacy. The wise saying goes, "You have to be in love to make love." If there is a gap between these two forms of intimacy, it often compromises the integrity of the relationship. Moreover, it validates the inevitable outcomes of men who use love for sex, and women who use sex for love. The end result is that these are two people who may have had the intention of falling in love, but now co-exist in a sex-based relationship. When sex is the foundation on which the relationship stands, it will eventually fail.

This chapter explores the significance of emotional and sexual intimacy in relationships. How important is sex for women? Is sex purely a form of intimacy to make a woman feel loved? The panel of women get to the core of these questions by discussing if it is possible to have a healthy relationship without sex. Members of the panel agree that the physical act of sex is a powerful form of intimacy, however, mental foreplay serves as a role of great significance to maintain the intensity of sexual intimacy. The women end the chapter talking about the emotional gratification of make-up sex.

Sex or No Sex? How Important Is It?

Angele

This is a good question. I do not think that it is possible to have a healthy relationship without sex. A couple might be able to have a "good" relationship, but not a "healthy" relationship. Sex is a healthy and integral part of a serious, committed relationship. In the quest to keep that commitment intact, a sexual anchor must be attached to the relationship. Other than that, a relationship without sex is nothing more than a friendship. If an individual is in a relationship with someone who "does not get their juices flowing" or "does not make them hot and bothered," then that person may not be "the one."

Last Valentine's Day, a group of girlfriends and I had a discussion on our "Anti-VDGNO" day (Valentine's Day-Girls Night Out). The conversation was cleverly summed up by a member of our group in this harsh and brutal manner: "A man is *not* 'the one,' if you are not willing to sexually please him in *every single* way possible." After reflecting on the statement along with some steamy, descriptive narratives, we all agreed. In order to be blissfully happy with a man, you have to be willing to give him what he wants sexually because chances are that what he wants is actually what he needs.

For most of my adult years, I valued sex more emotionally than physically. This resulted in several failed long-term relationships. I had an old-fashioned frame of mind. I thought before having sex with a man, it was first important to develop an emotional attachment. I thought having sex with a man meant we were in love and that love would last forever. I foolishly believed that our emotional bond would be stronger than our sexual bond. Because of this thought process, I preferred to hug, kiss, and cuddle, rather than, bang-bang all the time. I was of the opinion (and still am) that there is more to the art of intimacy than intercourse.

As a result of my decision to be more intimate than sexual, my past relationships fell into a routine of boredom. There was no steamy foreplay outside of the bedroom. There was no excitement inside of the bedroom. No spontaneous sex. No adventurous sex. No kinky sex. It was just the same boring routine. Thus, my boyfriends sought wild and crazy sex outside of the relationship and came home for predictable, missionary sex. They thought missionary sex was boring. I thought missionary sex allowed for intense body-to-body contact and a deeper level of intimacy that symbolized the act of making love. Their sex was disconnected and void of intimacy.

Alex

I do think it is possible to have a healthy relationship without sex. I actually prefer relationships that are not centered solely on a sexual connection. For me, a spiritual and emotional connection is much more important. I am of the opinion that a precursor needs to be in place to give the sex meaning. When a couple develops a spiritual and emotional connection, hopefully this will lead to them falling in love. Once in love, the couple is making love and not merely having sex.

In contrast, when sex is the center of the relationship, it is difficult to form a spiritual and emotional connection. Women and gay men need to know that coochie and moonchie will not keep a man. There is a plethora of that in the world. Yasss . . . I said, "plethora"! This is why it is mandatory to have some type of connection that is stronger than sexual intercourse.

Having said all of that, I know that in relationships I am often obligated to have sex (even more than I like to at times). The men who I have been in relationships with are obsessed with my sex. Yasss . . . You read that right. I would prefer to have sex once every two weeks. However, when in a relationship, I usually end up having sex 3-5 days a week. These men love my moonchie to death!

In all seriousness, I think sex can be a wonderful thing. However, it should not be the center of the relationship. There are a lot of myths about gay men as promiscuous, hypersexual beings who have sex with every Tom, Dick, and Harry. This is not true. The majority of gay men live a life of dignity and simply want to find another man who will love them and make them happy—— nothing more, nothing less.

Kenndi

I do believe that it is possible to have a healthy relationship without sex if both parties involved are on one accord: **No sex before love. Period.** In order for the relationship to flourish, it is extremely helpful that both people share the same belief system, which usually is the reason for the choice of abstinence.

I once dated an up-and-coming pastor for almost a year. During that time, God and my ex-boyfriend exposed me to many blessings. I had already been practicing abstinence for four years. None of the men I dated during that time had the same spiritual conviction about premarital sex and the importance of only having sex when two people are in love with each other. I found myself repeatedly defending my decision. It had become exhausting. When I was on the verge of feeling like Mother Teresa meets the Virgin Mary, I met "The Pastor" at my church home. One Sunday he came to be a guest pastor. I was also on the church program to sing a song titled, *Falling In Love With Jesus*. After my performance, he approached and said, "You have a lovely voice." I replied by thanking him and telling him that I as well enjoyed his sermon. He is a fiery, dynamic speaker. You could tell then that he was on the brink of doing great things.

In the eyes of the Lord and myself, he was beautifully created. He loved me, respected me, supported me, and understood my decision to practice abstinence. I told him that I was seeking clarity from God. This was a statement that I had made to previous boyfriends, however, they did not understand. My ex-boyfriends would ask, "How can I marry you without having sex with you?" I had to explain to them that in a marriage God created sex as a part of not only procreation, but also, the physical way two people express their love for one another. It was created to be a part of the marital bond. Sex was not created to be a gauge of whether two people should move from boyfriend/girlfriend to husband/wife. When sex is used only to satisfy the flesh, it is not an expression of true love.

My relationship with the pastor did not materialize to marriage. Our lives moved in separate directions when he joined a Christian mission program and I began a Ph.D. program. Our timing was off. Timing is the key to everything. God brought him into my life for a reason. It was to show me that I did not have to succumb to the pressure of sexually pleasing a man for him to love me unconditionally.

Camille

Relationships grow to become healthier when both parties have realistic expectations about sex. When two people are only dating, sex has the ability to complicate things. For this reason, I would highly suggest that individuals get to know each other before engaging in sexual intercourse. To make my point, my healthiest relationships have come from when my partner and I refrained from having sex for "X" period of time. Is the time frame two weeks? Is the time frame a month? Is the time frame three months? Is the time frame six months? Is the time frame a year? That is completely up to the two consenting adults. But with that being said, not all of the relationships lasted long enough to lead to sex, which made the decision to wait even better.

By comparison, in a marriage, sex is very important. It is not the most important aspect of my marriage, but it is not negotiable. We experience the occasional lull in frequency due to work, our children, or life in general, but we've never gone for an extended period without sex. We average about 2-4 times a week, which I am "Ok" with. If it is more, then that is great. If it is less, then that is a problem. In a marriage, there must be a sexual connection that stems from the emotional connection. For me, sex is a legitimate emotional need. For my husband, sex is a legitimate physical need. We both understand that.

Valerie

Sex is necessary to sustain a healthy relationship. It's important in any relationship, especially a healthy relationship, but it isn't detrimental if not present. To be clear, it's not detrimental if a couple practices abstinence or takes a break for a brief period of time. As a matter of fact, there are times when my husband and I have conflict in our marriage, have family-related stress, have work-related stress, etc., and simply opt out of the act of sex for a brief period. For example, after a heated conversation, we may shut down all intimacy—— emotionally and phys-ically. This is caused by our stubbornness or intent to "control" the in-timacy component in the relationship. He controls his "Johnson" and I control my "Cookie." There is no action, no sex. Eventually, we recon-cile our differences and the intimacy is revived.

It is important to keep the intimacy in the relationship vibrant. Couples should maintain an emotional closeness. This is imperative because at times the frequency of sexual activity will decline. In my marriage, we don't have a set schedule, like every Monday at 6:00 a.m. or Saturday at 8:00 p.m. It simply depends on the mood. Sometimes the level of intimacy is higher than others. For instance, we may have sex multiples times in one day or once a week. After being married for several years, I can admit that there have been times when we've only had sex once in a month. Yes, it sounds unbelievable, but it happens.

Could my husband and I survive without sex in our relationship? I'm sure we could, but we choose not to. We both know our love for each other is strong, and so to maintain the strength of that love, it is necessary to have an equally strong sexual connection. Our rela-tionship is like a boat. It is our love that keeps us afloat, but our sex, whether it's lovemaking, make-up sex, or chains and whips, rocks the boat. "Ahoy mate!"

The Art of Mental Foreplay

Angele

Mental foreplay is very important in a relationship. For me, foreplay is my partner *showing* his interest in me. It may be as simple as him showing empathy for how hard I worked that day and having a glass of wine ready when I walk through the door along with a romantic bath. Maybe it's him beginning the day with a text message that says nothing more than "Thinking of you, Babe" and a few hours later he sends me a photo of himself in a tank top to turn me on. Maybe it could be as elaborate as leaving small hints on pieces of paper around the house with instructions prior to making love. When I arrive home, the first hint will be posted on the front door. From that point on, the instructions are hidden around the house.

I absolutely love mental foreplay. For instance, I met a guy on the relationship website, *ChristianMingle.com*, about six months ago. He was a Christian, but he wanted to do more than just mingle. On about our fifth date, he invited me to go play pool. After a couple of glasses of wine, we began to place bets on the game. Bet #1: Go to the bathroom and remove your bra and place it in your purse. Bet #2: Go to the bathroom and remove your panties and hand them to me. Bet #3: I want you to ride on top of me on the ride home. The sexual wagers added more spice to our date. He stimulated my mind before he sexually pleased my body. The ride home was interesting to say the least.

Alex

Yasss! Mental foreplay is extremely important in a relationship. I want a man to make love to my mind as well as my body. Talk to me, honey! I want a man to give me life. I am attracted to intelligence. I want a man who can name all 44 presidents and can make executive decisions in the bedroom. I want a man who knows the Dows Jones is a stock market index as well as the nickname for my penis. I want a man who knows the difference between a "Whatchamacallit" and "Moonchie." Yasss . . . I want him to give me life . . . Be my everything! I want a man to mentally tease me to the point that my body is shaking.

One year while attending a Superbowl party, I was introduced to a heterosexual guy through mutual friends. He was standoffish at first, but after a few drinks he started to make eye contact with me. I giggled inside. I giggled because a lot of men are bi-curious but are not often in the right environments to satisfy their curiosity. He began the discussion asking about my desire to pursue a Ph.D. He had recently completed a dual M.D. and Ph.D. program at an Ivy League school. Since he was a doctor already, I wanted him to be my P.C.P. (Primary Care Physician or Professional Cock Pleaser). Your primary care doctor is your medical "home." I would love to come home to him every day. We talked and talked and talked. While everyone else was watching the football game, we were playing another kind of game. He was trying to "resist" while I was trying to "insist." We ended up going back to his condo that evening. There was no sex. We talked and talked and talked some more. We made out without touching. We had sex without touching. The bed-shaking finale was the hug at the end of the night.

Kenndi

Mental foreplay is incredibly important in a relationship. It sets the mood. It is the emotional precursor before the physical act of making love. Everything we do in life begins in the mind. When a woman's mind is stimulated, her body will follow suit and the result is nothing short of an organic experience between two people.

To mentally entice me, a man has to be an active listener. He has to challenge my mind to think. He has to ask stimulating and engaging questions that probe me to think outside of my comfort zone. To mentally entice me, I want to converse with a man who has an inner desire to be "great." I understand that this notion of "great" is ambiguous. In the words of Robert Baden-Powell, I want a man who will "Try and leave this world a little better than [he] found it." To mentally entice me, I want a man who holds Jesus Christ as the head of his life. When a man fits these criteria, it is much easier to feel comfortable engaging in a sexual relationship with him.

Camille

Mental foreplay is very important in a relationship. Foreplay is any non-physical action geared toward promoting sexual arousal. It requires the use of your own imagination. It can be played out throughout the entire course of the day, weeks, months, and even a year.

I have to tell this story. I know you are thinking—- weeks, months, and even a year? Yes. As I have said throughout, my sexual interactions with men have been mostly limited to serious, committed relationships and now in my marriage. I did a little here and a little there, but nothing to talk about. My friends would often make fun of me. They said, "You need to have a freak season." My reply was always, "No." I have had some fun but never had a freak season. Here is where mental foreplay can begin weeks, months, and even a year ahead of time.

I once friended this medical doctor on Facebook while in law school. I am always reluctant to accept the request of individuals who I do not personally know. We had more than 50 mutual friends, he was from my hometown, and I saw that he was doing some very positive things in the community, so I accepted. Yes, I cyberstalked him. He is an attractive and successful man. Weeks passed and every now and then he would "Like" one of pictures and comment on my posts. Four months passed and he inboxed me.

> Hi. I am glad to make your acquaintance. I see that we have some of the same friends. Do you know Cheryl? The two of you are in a couple of pictures together. That was one of my best friends in college. It sure is a small world. The reason for this communication is to ask you to come and speak to a group of doctors regarding FERPA laws. A few of your posts were in relation to the legality of such laws. I see that is one of your areas of expertise.

It was safe to say, he was cyberstalking me as well. It was cute. I took him up on the offer and spoke to the group of doctors. He compensated me for my services and sent a dozen roses to the law school. The card read, "Thank you for speaking to the group. It was a great presentation. Stay in touch." At this point, he had my full and undivided attention. However, more than two months had passed and I had not heard from him. I know what you're saying, "Why didn't you contact him?" I am old-fashioned.

My birthday was coming up in May. Two days before my birthday, he posted a happy birthday message on my Facebook wall. "Happy Early Birthday! I hope you have a wonderful day." Of course, I contacted several of my friends to decipher the message. One friend said it was just a general birthday message. Another friend said he wanted to take me out for my birthday. The last friend said to contact him and invite him out the day before my birthday. If he was lame, he wouldn't waste my time on my birthday. Again, I am old-fashioned. I did not contact him.

On the morning of my birthday, I arrived at the law school to see that he had sent me five dozens of roses, all colors. The receptionist said to me, "Someone really likes you." The card read, "I made reservations for us to have dinner tonight at Vic and Anthony's Steakhouse at 6 p.m." I had already made plans with my friends, however, they all encouraged me to go. That night we had a wonderful dinner. We talked and talked and talked. We drank and drank and drank. We were just two people enjoying the moment. The sexual tension between us was very intense. He hugged me, kissed me, undressed me, made sweet love to me, bathed me, and redressed me—— all with his eyes. At the end of the night, he hugged me like he was holding tight of the memory.

Valerie

Mental foreplay is extraordinarily important in a relationship. In my marriage, mental foreplay helps to ensure that our physical sex acts do not get old and stale. It keeps everything spicy, active, and alive—— inside and outside of the bedroom.

We both have wild and vivid imaginations; therefore, we look forward to the mental foreplay. Mental foreplay relieves our inhibitions in the bedroom and it alleviates any awkwardness when trying new positions, playing with new toys, and experimenting with different characters when role-playing. One of the things I like to do is talk and sext dirty messages to my husband. After a night of love making, I love to keep the fire burning by calling him on his way to work to remind him of the night before. I will ask, "Did you like the cheerleading uniform I wore last night?" Or, I will say, "I can't wait to feel you explode inside of me." Later in the day, I will sext him a picture of my vijayjay with a caption that reads, "She misses you?" He will reply, "I miss her, too!"

Both of our love languages are words of affirmation and physical touch. We are perfectly made for each other. Once while out at dinner, my husband experienced a "happy ending" at the table. I spoke softly and very explicitly to him across the table while intensely massaging his Johnson with my feet. He listened to me and vividly imagined the last time we made love. After dinner, we ventured into the bathroom at the restaurant and began another session of kinky fun. At the end of the day, we are both just sexual beings who love the intimacy of mental foreplay and lovemaking.

Make Up with Me

Angele

I absolutely love make-up sex. This type of sex has the ability to mask and help move beyond problems in the relationship. In my 40-plus years in this world, I have had plenty of make-up sex. Each time it gives me an automatic emotional reaction that the relationship will get back on the right path. Whether I believe it or not, my physical being wants to believe. My body wants to believe we are one. My body wishes that he would never leave us.

In a lot of ways, make-up sex is like having sex with your partner for the first time. It is emotionally driven. It is physically driven. The "make-up" part occurs because both parties have come to the agreement that neither one of you are ready to end the relationship. Once you come to that agreement, it is only right to re-consummate the relationship.

The last time I had make-up sex was mind-blowing. We hadn't seen each other in a month. Once we ended all the bickering, the conversation quickly turned into wanting to see each other ASAP. He was out of town on a business trip. The anticipation was killing me. We would call, text, sext, and masturbate over FaceTime while waiting for the next time our bodies would speak a language of love, lust, and forgiveness. I would text him messages that said, "Here is the lingerie that I am going to wear the next time we see each other." The lingerie was black with red ruffles around the breast area, a slit to expose my nipples, and an additional slit in the crotch area for him to gain easy access. He would reply, "I can't wait to see you!" We were two ticking time bombs ready to explode. When we finally saw each other, "Kaboom!" The emotionally driven make-up session helped to reacquaint our minds, bodies, and souls.

Alex

Make-up sex is always the best sex. Yasss . . . I said . . . Always. I really love a man who is sexually aggressive. The most aggression comes out during make-up sex. Aggression is always a turn on for me.

The last time my boyfriend and I had make-up sex, it was the Bomb Dot Com! The day before we were to see each other, he texted a series of questions:

Q: Would you rather it passionate or rough?
A: Both. Please start off passionately.

Q: Would you rather rope or handcuffs?
A: Both. Be creative.

Q: Would you rather candles or whip cream?
A. Both

Q: Would you like to role-play?
A. Yes, wear your police uniform. #GayLivesMatter

"I will be there at 9 a.m. when I get off of my shift," read his final text message. "Ok, see you then," I replied back excited like a little kid on Christmas Eve. I had to make sure everything was set.

Rope ☑

Whip cream ☑

Chocolate syrup ☑

Strawberries ☑

Moscato Wine ☑

'Sexual Healing' Music ☑

I was awake at 6:30 a.m. lying in bed dreaming about the morning ahead. I hopped out of the bed and immediately shaved. I wanted my face to match his bald, muscular chest. I then brushed my teeth. I wanted the menthol from the toothpaste to stimulate his loins. As the time approached, I put on some music. The first song was Robin Thicke, *Teach U A Lesson*. The song begins, "You feel so good/ You smell so good/ You feel so warm/ Just like I knew you would/ Can't let you go/ Can't let you go/ I can't let you go."

He texted me when he was outside of my apartment. That was his customary notice, "I'm outside. Please open the door." He loved when I would open the door and greet him naked. The display of excitement on my face always turned him on. When our eyes met, I could feel the passion in the air. His embrace was magnetic. Finally our lips touched, I closed my eyes, and traveled into another stratosphere. "You are gorgeous. I love you. I have missed you," he gently whispered in my ear. As he spoke those loving words into my left ear, all of the mean words he previously said to me exited out of my right ear.

"Sit right there," I requested of him while I walked over to the Bose player to restart the CD. "You feel so good/ You smell so good/ You feel so warm/ Just like I knew you would/ Can't let you go/ Can't let you go/ I can't let you go," echoed in the background. The make-up sex started off passionately, and then proceeded to be borderline psychopathic. I loved every bit of it.

Kenndi
Make-up sex is the best type of sex because there is a sense of emotional release. The emotions of make-up sex range from anger, outrage, to extreme and intense. Because of the level of its intensity, make-up sex is often viewed as the best type of sex. I am firmly of the opinion that the best way to end an argument is for my fiancé to throw me on the bed and make passionate love to me. Neither one of us wants to argue with each other. Both of us know that the argument is not going to lead to the end of the relationship. To circumvent the rigor of going through an unnecessary argument, please throw me on the bed and make passionate love to me.

The last time we had make-up sex was eye-opening. I had never seen him act like that before. We are both Christians, but he brought the devil into the bedroom that day. We were arguing about some non-sense. In the middle of the argument, he grabbed me close to him, kissed me, and threw me on the bed. I thought, here we go, traditional make-up sex. Nope. I was wearing a t-shirt and panties. He first ripped my t-shirt off. He then ripped my panties off. I was frozen. He turned me over and began spanking my ass. This is new, but I like it. He tied my hands behind my back with one of his bow ties. This is new, but I like it. He took a pillow and placed it under my pelvic area to elevate me for easier access. This is new, but I like it. I kept saying to myself, "The devil is a lie. The devil is a lie. The devil is a lie." I could feel my body trembling—— orgasm after orgasm. It felt so right and so wrong. This had to violate the Christian sex rules. God sees everything. I hope "He" wasn't looking at us right now. Damn! Damn! Damn! My fiancé kept telling me to relax. But I kept asking the Lord to deliver him. Eventually, I said a little prayer to myself, and that helped me to relax. That was the first day I had ever spoken in tongues.

Camille

Make-up sex is NOT the best type of sex. There was a time when I would have agreed that it was, but not anymore. It is difficult for me to have sex with my partner when I am angry, mad, or upset with him. I am a very sexual person, however, if there are other distractions in the relationship, it is difficult for me to channel my sexual energy.

My position on make-up sex has changed because I was once in a relationship where it seemed like all we had was "make-up sex." In most cases, it does not fix anything. The relationship was so bad that we would role-play in public in an attempt to reignite the love and commitment. For example, after a heated argument, I would always see him the next day in the gym.

This particular time he was on the elliptical machine. I made sure that his eyes and mine joined in unison. Shortly after seeing each other, we both made our way to the designated area to do sit-ups. "Hello, my name is Sterling," introducing himself. "My name is Sassi," I replied very gingerly. "Do you come here often? I've never seen you?" He said to drum up conversation. We would make small talk. Each of us was anxious to see who would be the first to break from their role.

We both finished our workout at the same time. Slowly approaching the front entrance of the gym, I could see Sterling slowly undressing me with his eyes. I wanted to grab him, throw him on the front counter, freeze time, and make love to him right then and there. But, I could not break my role. As we exited the gym, he handed me his business card. "Maybe we could go to dinner sometime," he suggested. We stared into each other's eyes for a couple of seconds but uttered no words.

When I arrived at work, my mind was useless. All I could think about was Sterling. I finally emailed him:

Hello Sterling. It was a pleasure meeting you today. Are you busy tonight? If not, maybe I can come over with a bottle of wine, and we can watch a movie. #NetflixAndChill

Call us crazy, but we took this role-playing sh!t to another level. There were days that it really worked to move our relationship forward. There were other days that we were just having fun awaiting the inevitable end.

Later that night, I arrived at his apartment. Knock! Knock! Knock! Sterling finally answered the door. He had just gotten out of the shower. Sterling answered the door with just a towel on. "Hi Sassi, you are early," he said while inviting me in. I had on a sundress with no bra and no panties. The "hot" phrase to our role-playing adventure was, "Do you find me attractive?" When either one of us would ask that question, it led straight to sex. I asked Sterling, "Do you find me attractive?" With a grin on his face, he replied, "Yes, I do. I find you very attractive." I then asked him, "Have you thought about having sex with me since we met today?" He nodded his head and said, "Yes, I have." These role-playing scenarios always led to the greatest make-up sex. In the end, we became great actors, but each of us failed in the leading role.

Valerie

Hands down, make-up sex is the best type of sex because my husband rocks me to the core, and shakes up my insides like an earthquake. I love it! During make-up sex, I see my husband in a different light, a good light. He becomes a different person, a more aggressive lover.

Once we have resolved our issues and enter the cooling period, the sexual frustration is high, almost unbearable. Let me set the scene:

With anticipation, we come home from work, eat dinner, and watch a little T.V. before turning in to prepare for work the next day. While in bed, lying in the dark, we both feel the sexual tension in the air. At this point, we've made up but are still cautious about touching each other. My heart starts to beat faster with each breath. I tell myself, "Take a deep breath. Be calm. This is your husband."

Like I said, my husband becomes a different person, a more aggressive lover. I'm never prepared for what happens next. Each time he catches me off guard. First, he will forcefully pull off my silk short set. Then he will forcefully pull off my panties. His behavior is aggressive, almost dominatrix-like. In these moments, I love being submissive. Some times he will use the bed restraints to tie me to the bed, place a gag in my mouth, and blindfold me. He will then chastise me for my actions. "You have been a bad girl!" "Why don't you ever listen to me?!" "Daddy has to punish you!" The more he talks, the more I am turned on. The rougher he gets, the more I am turned on. The force of his penetration is the best feeling ever. He is so hard and deep that I can feel my uterus flipping. I can feel his penis touching the tip of my ovaries. My husband is well-endowed. Therefore, in moments like this, I just pray that he is careful. But, my prayers often fall on deaf ears. This is the only time I do not want my prayers to be answered. Three words, "Thank you, Jesus!"

Chapter 5

Dear Thomas, Dear Paisley,
Dear Thomas, Dear Jamison

The shattering of a heart when being broken is the loudest quiet ever. ~Carroll Bryant

Dear Thomas,

You are my husband and I love you. This is the most painful letter that I have ever had to write in my life. Despite the constant tears that stream while writing, I will try to make my way through it. You and I have been on this emotional roller coaster for nearly two decades—— the ups and downs have taken their toll—— afraid of the big fall. Sadly, there have been more downs than ups. Through it all, we have somehow persevered behind this perfect façade. During this marriage, both of our emotional states have been tested often affecting how we have behaved toward one another. These emotions are the reason for this letter—— disappointment, frustration, anger, sadness, and resentment—— all of which have led me to sit down and put these words on paper.

Over the years, we have created a beautiful family. As the saying goes, "It's the love of family that makes life beautiful." I love you. I love our kids. I love our family. Watching the kids grow from babies to young adults has been very fulfilling. It has provided a special joy and sadness. Looking at them makes me reflect back to when we first met. It truly seems like yesterday.

We both worked at Sam's Club. You were a supervisor and I was newly hired. Separated by the fear of romance in the workplace and an eight-year age gap, I was concerned that a relationship between a supervisor and subordinate would not be in our best interest. However, you made it clear that you were interested in dating me (and nothing would stop us from being together). I was immediately drawn to your smile, confidence, ambition, and wisdom.

I was just getting out of a relationship and very skeptical about dating anyone, especially an older man. My ex-boyfriend hurt me. He lied, cheated, and verbally abused me. As an older man, it appeared that you were past the childish games. You seemed more mature, selfless, and stable. You told me things I'd never heard before. You showed me things I'd never seen before. You made me feel a way I'd never felt before. Some of my innocence and purity was still in tact. You appreciated that. But, that was the most disconcerting. I did not want you to be my guinea pig as I tried to figure out the type of man I wanted, what I wanted to do with my life, and whether I was actually in love with you. You took care of me. You made me feel secure. I have never had to worry since the day I met you. I married you because I felt in my heart that you would be a great husband.

Here we are years later. While I appreciate all you have done for our family, you have made some grave mistakes along the way. First, I know you have not always been faithful. The late nights with your friends, guy's trips, visits to the strip club, extended business trips, and me periodically checking your cell phone, helped me place all of the pieces of infidelity in the puzzle. I knew about Breana from Houston, Johnnie Lynn from New Orleans, Cassie from Baton Rouge, Edith from Oxnard, Maddie from Wichita, Kristy from Raleigh, Mona from D.C., and Shannon from Atlanta. Having knowledge of these affairs over the years, I initially blamed myself for living in their shadows. There were many nights I contemplated leaving, but I couldn't leave. I would lay in the bed emotional, but motionless. A lot of emotions and thoughts surfaced—— loneliness, fear, time invested, lack of financial security, and regret. The thought of starting over scared me. I was afraid to travel the journey alone. Many rhetorical questions were posed. However, the main questions were: How long can I pretend to be happy? Would the next relationship bring eternal happiness?

Like I said, for the longest time I blamed myself. I got so caught up in enjoying the financial security, working, raising the kids, and trying to finish graduate school, that I often wondered if I had neglected you in some way(s) that would make you want to have multiple affair. But despite knowing your actions, I never considered cheating on you. Despite you having set very strict parameters for me, I never considered cheating on you. I could not have any single friends. I could not hang out with work friends nor attend after-work functions. I had to be home at a certain time. You would call and text while I was in class. Sometimes you would show up at my class unannounced. God forbid if I had any free time, you would request that the kids accompany me. Despite all of that, I never considered cheating on you.

Over time you seemed threatened by my emerging independence and pursuit of a career. Yet, I was still a prisoner to your controlling ways. To be honest, I did not mind for the longest time. My mind would not allow me to hate, resent, or question your motives. Of course we had our arguments about it, but my larger focus was on keeping our family together and making sure the kids grew up in a stable environment. All of that changed the day I met "him."

Before meeting him, I didn't even look at another man. Why? Because you had me petrified to even look. I didn't make eye contact with male co-workers while working on projects. I walked with my head down everywhere I went—— grocery store, mall, etc. You ingrained in my mind the idea that because I was attractive, guys would flirt with me and make advances. Then ultimately, I would make a decision that would break up our family. You repeatedly told me, if we ever got a divorce, it would be my fault. I use to laugh inside knowing you had a Rolodex of women at your disposal. Knowing that you were actively cheating, you shifted the blame for your actions on me and attempted to make me feel like I was capable of destroying our family. The whole time you were enjoying life in every way possible.

Thomas, I wanted to enjoy life as well. I had a good life, but I was not happy. Frankly, it was never my intention to cheat on you. I do not believe in an "eye for an eye." I wanted to be the person in this marriage who could forever say I upheld my vows, which was, "to be faithful for as long as we both shall live." I can no longer say that. I did not cheat for revenge; I cheated to reclaim my life. You never gave me the chance to be me. You tried your best to control me. You fell out of love with me a long time ago. Afterwards, you became a dictator— controlling, selfish, and very mean at times. You hugged me like a complete stranger. You kissed me like our lips had never met. You made love to me like you did not love me. To that end, you pushed me into another man's arms.

His name is irrelevant. Where we met does not matter. All I need you to know is that I loved him. I really loved him. At times when I looked at him, I thought I saw the man who I was supposed to marry. He was my long lost soul mate. However, I knew that we could never be together and that was incredibly painful. There was a time in this whole ordeal that I truly contemplated walking away from our marriage. He came into my life when I had reached "the big fall" and provided "true happiness." His presence gave me the emotional drive to do the things that I had always wanted to do, and provided a certain level of happiness that was not dependent upon you.

I loved how he looked at me, how he listened to me, how we laughed together, how we could discuss things about the kids that you did not care about, and how it seemed that he cared about every element of my life. I loved how he gave me long hugs, how he would grab my face and kiss me, how he would write me love letters, how he would send me songs, how he would tell me how much he loved me (a lot), how he would make me feel loved, and more important, how he made me feel like the most important woman in the world. All this was done and we *never* once had sex— the true act of making love. Our interactions were based on love, affection, openness, transparency, and a mutual understanding of the type of love we both desired from a partner.

On the other hand, I was sad because I had alienated you. I was involved with another man, and while he made me extremely happy, that happiness came with a very high cost— the highest being my conscience. I could not ignore my conscience. I was not selfish enough to continue to cheat. I had become you. But, I am not you. All the nights I would lay in bed crying myself to sleep wondering what you were doing, had now transitioned to crying myself to sleep because of what I was doing to you, the kids, and to myself.

The world is not perfect. In a perfect world, I'd be with him and not you. In all of this, I've learned that we forgive in order to continue on a path to obtain happiness. I could not leave you and the kids. There is where my happiness lies. Thomas, I am very sorry that I fell out of love with you and in love with another man. I am very sorry. I know that it may be difficult to forgive me for my actions, but I believe you must. I have forgiven you many times. Believe it or not, I do not want a divorce. I want to reconcile our marriage. I would like for us to start anew. This time I want us both to honor the vows of our marriage. Lets start with counseling, and proceed to practice the habits of communication, respect for each other, and every day work on making our marriage better.

Love,
Paisley

Dear Paisley,

You are my dear wife. I appreciate your honesty and sincerity in your letter to me. I appreciate that more than you will ever know. I read your letter over and over trying to figure out where things went wrong with us. After sitting and thinking, I put my finger on what caused us to go down this path of unhappiness and betrayal of each other.

We have had some ups and downs in our relationship, but I disagree with you when you said there were more downs than ups. We had a very good relationship in the beginning. I believe we had a relationship that was predicated on your happiness. What I mean by that is, as long as you were happy, I was happy. I think me being older than you may have created a situation where I felt somewhat responsible to ensure that you followed certain steps to achieve happiness and life success. It was sort of like how a father would mold his daughter.

I know that my controlling ways were not good for our relationship, but I felt like I needed to protect you and that was my way of doing that. I almost felt like you would wake up one day and realize you were too good for me and decide to leave. I always felt like I was out of your league. I guess trying to keep you under lock and key was my way of trying to stop you from seeing that there was possibly someone out there better for you than me.

The turning point of our relationship began when we became parents. We were and are great parents. However, before we became parents, we were a couple. We were that for nearly five years before our first child. Those were what I would call our glory years. We had fun and lots of it. We took it for granted that the fun would continue after having children. Neither one of us put in the extra work needed to maintain our couple status. I will take full responsibility for my part. We both put all of our efforts into being the best parents we could be (and we should have). We have succeeded in that area but our relationship as a couple has been on life support for years.

The drive we both had to be good parents drove each of us in different directions, me to the streets and you into the arms of another man. I can admit I sought happiness in other places. You loved the children more than you loved me. The ironic thing about this is that we both were looking for the same thing, the attention that we felt we were not getting at home. With all that being said and everything being laid out on the table, I think we are a long ways from being the fairy tale that we had been hiding behind for all of these years. I guess the only question that needs to be answered is, are we going to make this marriage work?

We have both made mistakes. Your willingness to reconcile shows me the level of commitment that you have not only to our family but to me as well. My desire is to be happy again. That happiness contains you and the children. We are a family. As you stated in your letter, the world is not perfect. You are not perfect. I am not perfect. But, we are perfectly made for each other. If you are willing to forgive me, I am willing to forgive you as well. We can start anew. Thank you for believing in us and what we have built together.

Love,
Thomas

Dear Thomas,

I read your letter. Thank you very much for understanding. Thank you for believing in us. Thank you very much for wanting to make our marriage work. That means the world to me.

I promise to do a better job at showing my love for you. While I understand that the golden rule of motherhood is to love our kids more than our spouse, I must do a better job at dividing that love equally. This whole situation has shown me that my bond with the kids is unbreakable, however, my bond with you is fragile. Our bond should be just as strong. As you said, we are a family. I want to do any and every thing to make sure our family stays grounded in love and understanding.

Thomas, I ask that we never cheat on each other again, neither physically nor emotionally. You hurt me and I hurt you. We should never hurt each other. I do not want our kids to see the effects of an unhappy home and failed marriage.

I love you and will always love you.

Love,
Paisley

Dear Jamison,

I hope all is well in your world. I want to tell you in this letter that my husband and I have decided to make our marriage work.

I am sorry to write you this letter. I need to release these feelings from my heart. Each day that I inch closer to putting the idea of "us" to rest— is like grieving a death— the pain— is indescribable. I recognize that you were not (nor should you have been) vested in "us" as much as I was. Spending time with you was never a getaway from the pain and misery of my marriage. I often replay the time we spent together over and over again in my mind. I hear the words we spoke in my mind and it all seems surreal. Did that really happen? Did I really fall in love with another man? Will I ever fall out of love with him? How could a man whose only made love to my mind, and not my body, make me feel this way? Do I really have to let him go? The answer to all of these questions is, "Yes." It is time to move on. When I come to that same realization time and time again, the pain sets in. It is brutal.

Jamison, I have been in mourning. I have been in mourning due to an act of selfishness that was not set in the natural order of love. All of my love should have went to my husband. However, I gave his love to you and deceived the process of allowing our love to heal. Granted, my husband lied to me, he cheated on me, and he fell out of love with me. When he lied, I should have confronted him. But, I was afraid to break up my family. When he cheated, I should have shown the proof of his actions. But, I was afraid to break up my family. When he fell out of love with me, I should have pressured him even more to seek marriage counseling. He refused counseling and said, "The problem is you and not me." I told him, "If I have a problem, we have a problem." That statement fell on deaf ears. I never mentioned marriage counseling again. I was afraid to break up my family.

When we met, I was lost emotionally. You were available when I needed love. You were a friend when I needed a best friend. You listened when I needed someone to listen. You were a shoulder when I needed to cry. You were present when he was absence. For that, I thank you very much.

In reflection, I have asked God, why did 'He' bring you into my life? Why would 'He' allow me to fall in love with you, for me to have to eventually tell you, our loveship needed to end? I have no answers. All I have are questions. Despite me having to discontinue our loveship, I do not regret meeting you, knowing you, and loving you. Eventually, I will learn and grow from this experience.

I continue to wish you the best. May God bless you forever.

Love,
Paisley

Chapter 6

Poems of Expression

Love is so short, forgetting is so long. ~Pablo Neruda

Negative Energy

Our thoughts direct the flow of energy/ Positive/ Negative/ Or indifferent/ I tried to destroy the energy you transferred to me/ But it lies dormant in the center of my heart/ A hostage to the kinetic force field/ Which makes you believe you can walk in and out of my life energy free/

Every day I pray for your happiness/ Because when you are happy, I am happy/ Every day I pray you are not sad/ Because when you are sad, I am sad/ I've cried for you, to absolve your pain/ And I've cried because of you, hoping that I will never see you again/

I am a prisoner to your negative energy/ An inmate/ You violated the basic laws of physics/ Despite not being complicit/ Life still sentenced me for aiding and abetting/ For not defusing your energy/

Objective reality/ You were not who I thought you were/ My love for you connected me to a false truth/ The battle between a strong mind and a fragile heart/ Is a difficult war to win/ Your conservation of energy ended our relationship/ Protecting your heart/ And wounding my heart forever/
~Hoston, 2015

The Unknown

There is a reason why Elephants are scared of bees/ The sound of fear is frightening/ There is nothing to fear but fear itself/ Falling in love takes the strength of letting go of fear/

There is a reason why Bees do not have ears/ And Flies are deaf/ They both co-exist in a world/ That hears no evil/ The outside noise can rescind the inside love/

There is a reason why love is my guide/ My love for you is as large and strong as an Elephant/ Even in the midst of fear/ Blinded by the sight of my conscience/ Deaf to the sound of dissent/ We exist/ Because love is a compass that directs our emotions to find happiness/ Even amongst imperfect circumstances/ I love you/
~Hoston, 2015

Pretty Tomboy

The bumps and bruises on your knees have healed over time/ Back then, you kept falling and falling and falling off of your bike/ You carried him on the handle bars/ And them in the child safety seats/ It is unbelievable how you pedaled up the hill/ The strength of love is amazing/ But the weight of love takes a toll/

No training wheels were needed for you/ You started riding at a young age/ Now in your older years/ You have put the training wheels on your new bike/ Because the ride is different/ The trail is unknown/ Little do you know, the path to happiness leads many to redefine their journey/ This time you won't fall/ Life will hold you up/ No more bumps and bruises for the Pretty Tomboy/
~Hoston, 2015

Clouds Are Formed to Cry Tears

Clouds are formed to cry tears/ Some days the sun shines through/ Other days tears fall down into the cracks of the pavement/ A place where broken hearts go to mend/ Hoping for someone, something/ To brighten their lives/

Broken people often find each other/ Either to put each other back together/ Or shatter the remaining pieces/ Consequently, the cracks of the pavement is no place to find love/ But when I stepped on a piece of broken glass/ I realized another heart had broken here before my own/

This raises the questions/ Do hearts always break?/ Do the pieces crystallize into peace?/ In the cracks of the pavement, is there a broken existence or a rainbow?/
~Hoston, 2015

Which Day Is It?

He broke up with me on a Monday

He took me to church on Sunday/ Made love to me on Saturday/ Sent a card, flowers, and candy to my job on Friday/

My life is in a backwards spiral

In the card, he wrote, "I will always love you./ I cannot imagine my life without you."/ That was just three days ago/

On Tuesday/ He called and asked, "Are you ok?/ "How are you handling the breakup?"/ The day after he broke up with me/

My life is at a standstill

On Wednesday/ He called and said he reconsidered his decision/ His love for me is unconditional/ He then asked could we try again/ I agreed/

On Thursday/ I broke up with him/ Three days after he broke up with me/ I am human/

My life is moving forward
~Hoston, 2015

Her Reflection Is Distorted

Me speaking to her:

I hope you are seeing your own reflection in the water/ Shallow waters can cast distorted images/ The more you see/ The less you observe/ The paradox of life/ The view is often a contradiction/ Abstract/ In the search for concrete answers/ We only see what we know/ Which questions everything we know/ We know nothing/

You love me/ And I love you/ But Thou Shalt Not . . . / Which makes it difficult for us to see each other/ The consequence of living between two worlds/

You have become the loneliest whale in the sea/ Communicating at a frequency not used by any other/ It is unfortunate that no one else hears your cries/ Except for the Lord and me/

When the waters calm/ I hope a new, yet, more accurate reflection of yourself will emerge/ Your beautiful self/
~Hoston, 2014

Let This Day Stand . . .

Let this day stand as our closure

This time/ Will be the last time/ After we leave each other's presence/ There will be no more/ No more hugs/ No more kisses/ No more conditional love/ No more us/ Our lives will move forward/ Unfortunately/ It will move in separate directions/

Let this day stand as our closure

We arrived at this place in our lives by mistake/ But we will leave here on purpose/ For the longest time/ Neither one of us wanted to make *the* decision/ However, not making a decision/ Is ultimately making a decision/ Because of that, the decision needed to be made/ That we both must move on/ No longer holding onto what "He" was asking us to walk away from/

Let this day stand as our closure
~Hoston, 2016

ABOUT THE AUTHORS

LATOSHA M. DUFFEY, also known as DJ Duffey, is a well-known Disk Jockey, author, motivational speaker, and activist from Dallas, Texas. Ms. Duffey has spoken on numerous panels concerning women's rights, breaking into male-dominated professions, and building a brand while being a wife and mother. She is currently working on a memoir titled, *Women Who Run the World*. Ms. Duffey's motto is, "Do what you love, surround yourself with people who make you happy, and stand up for what you believe in." Once she adhered to these words, everything in her life changed for the better.

For more information on Ms. Duffey, please visit:
www.iwantdjduffey.com

DR. WILLIAM T. HOSTON, Sr., Ph.D., is a professor, author, motivational speaker, poet, and documentarian who hails from New Orleans, Louisiana. He is associate professor of political science at the University of Houston—Clear Lake. Dr. Hoston holds research interests in the areas of minority voting behavior, political behavior of Black politicians, race and minority group behavior, Black masculinity, sexualities and gender, race and crime, and theories and dynamics of racism and oppression. He has penned a total of nine books, most recently, *Race and the Black Male Subculture: The Lives of Toby Waller* (2016), *RNIT* (2015), *Listen to Me Now, or Listen to Me Later: A Memoir of Academic Success for College Students, 2nd Edition* (2014), *Black Masculinity in the Obama Era: Outliers of Society* (2014), and *No Bullies in the Huddle* (2013).

For more information on Dr. Hoston, please visit:
www.williamhoston.com

www.ingramcontent.com/pod-product-compliance
Lightning Source LLC
Chambersburg PA
CBHW072012170626
46813CB00005B/2124